I SEE BUILDINGS FALL LIKE LIGHTNING

ALSO BY

KEIRAN GODDARD

Hourglass

Keiran Goddard

I SEE BUILDINGS FALL LIKE LIGHTNING

Europa
editions

Europa Editions
27 Union Square West, Suite 302
New York NY 10003
www.europaeditions.com
info@europaeditions.com

This book is a work of fiction. Any references to historical events,
real people, or real locales are used fictitiously.

Copyright © 2024 by Keiran Goddard
First publication 2024 by Europa Editions

All rights reserved, including the right of reproduction
in whole or in part in any form.

The right of Keiran Goddard to be identified as the author of this work
has been asserted by him in accordance
with the Copyright, Design & Patents Act 1988.

Library of Congress Cataloging in Publication Data is available
ISBN 979-8-88966-008-8

Goddard, Keiran
I See Buildings Fall Like Lightning

Lines from "La Barcarola Termina" ("The Watersong Ends") on p. 170
taken from Pablo Neruda: *Selected Poems*, Translated by Anthony Kerrigan
(Houghton Mifflin, 1990)

Cover design and image by Ginevra Rapisardi

Cover image: collage of Unsplash images

Prepress by Grafica Punto Print—Rome

Printed in Canada

CONTENTS

One - 15
Two - 59
Three - 95
Four - 165
Five - 185

Acknowledgements - 207

In memory of Craig McGill
(1984–2002)

The world is the closed door. It is a barrier.
And at the same time it is the way through . . .
every separation is a link.
—Simone Weil, *Gravity and Grace*

I SEE BUILDINGS FALL LIKE LIGHTNING

One

Rian

And then none of it happened. All of the lives we were sure we would have. All of the freedom and the fever. None of it happened. And now we are here. Tonight.

Nights like these usually go the same way. Drink with the old lads in the Trident, call in a few grams and then head into town. It's been the same for a decade or more. The same ever since we've had enough cash between us for things like taxis and completely unnecessary rounds of sweet, sticky shots. I'm not bored of it though. It's easy. Mindless. Month to month, day to day, my life isn't like that. My life isn't easy. My life is heavy. Even the nice things in my life are heavy. The restaurants all feel heavy, the drinks all feel heavy, even my fucking pen is heavy. I like a heavy watch. A heavy watch is fair enough. But who needs a heavy pen?

Tonight there is a different plan, for at least two reasons. Oli is thirty. Oli. Alive. Thirty years old. Thirty fucking years old. Something about that doesn't feel right at all. But it needs celebrating, marking, so that is what we will do. When I think of Oli he is in aspic, fifteen for ever. Fifteen with shiny skin, fifteen with bright white trainers, fifteen and always asking to go halves on a cigarette, fifteen with a knack for only ever asking when you're down to your last one. And now he's lived long enough to be fifteen twice over. Something about that doesn't feel right at all.

So Oli's mom has got involved and rented the back room of the Trident. A minor variation on the usual plan, granted, but not an entirely insignificant one. It will mean she's paid for it, for a start, which I know she can't afford. There will be cold food on one side of the room and she'll make us wait until nine until we can eat. And it will mean that either the rest of Oli's family will be there, which will make him feel uncomfortable, or the rest of Oli's family won't be there, which will make him feel devastated, even if he denies it.

The other issue is that Oli is our mate, practically our brother, but he's also our dealer. What's the etiquette? Doesn't feel right to text a man during his own birthday party and ask him to bring enough stuff to liven up the night. I'm hoping Patrick will have thought about this ahead of time and sorted it out.

It's the type of thing he might do. He's always been the cleverest. And the kindest. He's the best of us. Bit sanctimonious these days, but still, he's the best of us.

Oh, and there's something else as well. Oli is our mate, and our brother, and our dealer, but he's also an addict. Which is properly depressing. The lad looks worse every time I see him. That's the main issue with the family thing. They've tried with him, but he's really hard to help and I know it's difficult for them to watch. Thirty fucking years old. Something about that doesn't feel right at all.

Before the drugs, Oli was beautiful. Or striking. Or whatever the word is. He still is to me, to us, but before the drugs, he was that way to everyone. As a kid he seemed like some sort of thoroughbred horse who'd wandered onto the estate by accident. Better skin, for one thing, always tanned even though we all went months without seeing the sun. He looked muscular before any of the rest of us, and his hair was always better too. We had all cycled through every shit haircut you could imagine over the years, but Oli never bothered. He kept it long, flecked brown like MDF, just skimming his eyes. It always looked good, even when it seemed massively out of fashion and would have looked genuinely offensive if any of us had tried it.

His hair is still like that. Bit thinner, bit greasier, but basically the same. A few months back, I went round to his and if I'm honest, for the first time, you really had to squint to see his beauty. His body had thinned right out. The poor fucker looked a bit like a baseball bat with a sad face drawn on it. He'd got himself a dog, which seemed like a stupid idea to me. But Oli seemed proud of the dog, so I let it lick my hand and leave that thick gone-off-soup smell on my fingers. At some point the dog got bored and started trying to eat a fly that had landed on the coffee table. I can't really explain why, but watching that dog lap at that tiny fly with its fat, inaccurate tongue was probably even worse than seeing Oli looking the way he did.

Whenever I come back, I try to stay in a hotel just outside the city. It's a habit I've picked up. I'm weird about it. I like to be near the city, but not in the city, and high enough up that I can see almost the whole of it from my window. I think it is something about needing to see the shape of a place, which parts of it are tallest, which parts of it look oldest, which parts look like they might be dying and which parts look like they might be about to spring into life. How can you know somewhere if you only ever look at it from the inside out?

I check in late, drop my bag in the room without even turning on the light; it will take a while to get back to the estate from this end of town and I don't want to miss the first few rounds. The first few rounds set the tone; if you don't get them right it can be hard to pull things back from the fire. The last thing I want is for the shape of the night to set before it has really got started. I've seen it happen enough times over the years, Conor already darkening like a ripe bruise that will never heal, Patrick not able to stop himself bringing the injustices of the world back from the bar with him. Not tonight. Tonight we walk the wire and tonight nobody falls.

The taxi winds its way through the sprawl. The last light of the day is loosening its grip, disclosing, confessing, opening its hands, letting the new night tumble out through its fingers.

Patrick

We used to have a library. A building with books in it. But then the money ran out, or the money went missing, or the money was never there to begin with, so the building became a van. A van with books in it. A van with books in it that we called the book van.

For a few years, once a week, the book van came to our school. We would get to go in two at a time and pick something from a pile of books that seemed to get smaller every time. With hindsight, some little fuckers must have been stealing from the book van. Tragedy of the commons, I suppose.

One morning we heard that some older kids had set the book van on fire. Rian claimed that it was his cousin who had done it. I can't remember now if I believed him. But I do remember being sad that somebody had set the book van on fire and wondering whether it had burned quicker because of all the paper. And I also remember sort of wishing I could have seen it burn. At that point in my life, I'm not sure I'd ever seen anything on fire that wasn't actually *meant* to be on fire.

Next time I see Rian, next time I'm sitting in his expensive car that is so dark green that most of the time it looks black, I am going to ask him whether he remembers the book van. My guess is that even if he does remember it, he will say that he doesn't. Rian doesn't like to talk about the time before he was rich. Back when people had cars that were *either* green *or* black. Back when not every single fucking thing had to be a "hybrid" or a "blend."

Now that he's rich, months pass between Rian coming home: three, sometimes four at a push. And when I say home, I mean that it is home for the rest of us. I have no idea if he still thinks of it like that. With Rian, you get the sense that he is always moving, buying things somewhere and then selling the same things somewhere else. He once told me that the things he most liked to buy and sell were the things that had always existed and that nobody could make more of. Things like stone and land and metal. I think about that quite a lot.

He sends gifts. Aftershave in old-fashioned bottles. And whisky, also in old-fashioned bottles. Rian seems to love old-fashioned bottles. The gifts arrive in tatty boxes with interesting stamps on them. If the stamp is from Japan then I picture Rian in Japan, if the stamp is from Switzerland then I imagine him there. I know this isn't an accurate method. Things take ages to arrive in the post, and he is probably long gone by the time the boxes get to us. It's a bit like that thing you learn when you're a teenager, about how the light from stars takes so long to reach earth that you're always looking at a star that is already long dead. But less morbid. Or less romantic. Depending on how you feel about dead stars.

Whenever Rian is back, we get fucked up. Every time. He'll only be around for forty-eight hours or so, and nine times out of ten we won't sleep for the whole weekend. Usually, a group of us will meet in the Trident, which is the only pub left on the estate. The Trident is a shit pub. And it has a flat roof. The flat roof is important. Not all shit pubs have flat roofs, but all pubs with flat roofs are shit. Wisdom. Anyway, we'll meet there and drink pint after pint of cheap, cold, fizzy lager. Which, if people could be honest for more than ten seconds at a time, would still be accepted as the best type of lager. Expensive lager tastes like licking dirty wood.

So we do that. Drink with the old lads in the Trident. Men who have known our dads or our uncles, men who tell the same few stories on a loop, setting one another up for punchlines they've been honing for decades. We do this until about ten, at which point someone texts Oli to bring us a few grams before we get a taxi into town. That is always the worst part of the night for me. Not fucked up enough to have stopped caring. Feeling like maybe we're a bit old to be going to clubs. Feeling like my crap clothes might make me look a bit of an idiot. Worrying about spending money I don't really have.

I need to make something clear. None of us resent Rian being successful. Despite the ethics of it all, there is still a part of me that is almost proud of him. He was always obsessed with making money, even when we were kids. Running scams at school, buying cans of Coke from the shop in the morning and then selling them for a mark-up at break time when we were all thirsty from playing football in our uniforms. And he just carried on like that. He never stopped. When the rest of us were getting into girls, or music, or drugs, Rian just carried on. Buying things. Selling things.

I don't buy things or sell things. I deliver things. I deliver things for a living. I deliver things in order to live. People buy food from restaurants and I get paid eight quid an hour to ferry the food from the restaurant to their house on my bike. All the adverts for the company I work for show pictures of Thai food or sushi, as if that is what I spend hours carrying about. But it's not. I've never once carried sushi or Thai food. It's almost always a cheap, greasy burger that has basically fallen apart by the time I hand it over to the grateful, tired-looking bastard who ordered it. When they open the door to me, they usually seem a bit ashamed of how they look, or how their house looks, or about the fact they can't or won't give me a tip, even though it's pouring with rain and they know they probably should.

I'm out on the edge of something that is crumbling, scratching out a living, watching a system crack at the joints. A treadmill stuck on a setting that is too high. Trying to get a steady footing, trying to breathe. Praying I'll live long enough to watch the whole thing burn, hoping we can build something better from the rubble. But willing to take the risk either way.

I don't buy things. Or sell things. Other than my time. I suppose I sell that. And my body. Which, incidentally, is breaking apart pretty quickly these days. I deliver things. For a living. I deliver cold burgers, mostly.

Shiv

When Patrick calls, I can hear Oli jabbering away in the background, asking the taxi driver to turn up the radio. I know what Patrick will say before he even says it. They will have decided not to stay at the Trident until closing and to head into town to carry on the night instead . . . *yeah, I know I said I'd be home, but it's Oli's night and I think he's keen to dance off his buffet food . . . you know what he's like . . . give Molly and Freya a kiss goodnight from me?*

I don't mind. I'm glad to be at home tonight. I've lost the habit of going out and the prospect of an awkward buffet in the backroom of the pub isn't enough to tempt me out of retirement, as much as I love Oli. Even if I did fancy it, it's fifty quid for a babysitter that we definitely can't afford or tapping up my mom to take care of the girls for the night, which I know she's not really up to these days. It's good to have her just down the road, somewhere to go to borrow a tenner or to stay for a couple of days on the odd occasion Patrick and I need a bit of space. But she's not got the energy she used to. Bad legs, she says, or bad bones. But I think there might be something else going on. Something coming to an end.

And anyway, I like these hours alone, while the girls are asleep and Patrick is out. There's a quietness that settles over the flat, an almost sensual joy in walking from room to room, knowing they will be empty, flicking off every light one by one, the darkness seeming to make everything even quieter still. You shouldn't trust people who choose light over the gloom, in the same way that you shouldn't trust people who prefer clear blue skies to skies brimful of clouds. Clouds can change shape, transform; they can look like dogs and then like feet and then like a smiling, benevolent god and then like a smiling, sarcastic god and then like a smiling, vengeful god, all in the space of a minute. But clear blue skies are just blue, and clear. It's the same thing with the darkness: who would want to sit at home with the lights on, staring at the same furniture and walls they have seen a thousand times already that day? On nights like this, when I get the chance, I'll always choose the shadows and the silhouettes.

I know I'm supposed to want more than this. To want a life that's bigger somehow, but I really don't know what that means any more. Mostly when people say it, I think they actually just mean I should get a job. And for what?—to break my back and my mind at a warehouse or a call centre and then hand all of the money over to the people who are looking after Molly and Freya? There might be places in the world where that equation makes sense, but this place isn't one of them. We tried it for a year or so but the only work that really fitted around the girls' schedule was home working, getting paid by the piece to glue the slats of wooden lampshades together. Despite what the company said, nobody with a normal number of fingers could assemble them quick enough to make the whole thing worthwhile. That's without taking into account the fact that your money got docked for every lampshade you ruined, which was a fair amount, or the fact that you had to submit to living a life constantly surrounded by piles of balsa and wood glue. Fuck it, frankly. There's texture to my days and it's a small mind that can't see it. Universe in a grain of sand, heaven in your hand and all that.

Sometimes people don't believe me, but I don't want a tiny dog or a kitchen island or a private island or an ugly car or somebody else in my space, following me around and cleaning up my rubbish. I joke with Patrick sometimes, a riff well worn over the years . . . *anyway, who do I ask? Is there a government department or an online questionnaire I can fill in that will help me figure out what counts as a meaningful life, a life not wasted?* The answer would always be the same, wouldn't it? Your life was probably fine, but it wasn't what it could have been. You were never quite yourself, but you never quite managed to escape yourself either. It's not that I don't give a fuck. I care about being able to live freely, about clean air, about a peaceful world. But I don't want to spend my days grappling ghosts the way Patrick sometimes does. I admire him, I really do, and I get it, the sky is falling, we all know that, but we've got to live, there aren't many other options on the table.

There's something else about Oli's birthday as well. A memory it dredges up every time, small but shameful. We must have all been about fifteen—me, Patrick, Oli, Conor, Rian—laughing our way through lessons, distracted by in-jokes and petty dramas that always seemed to expand to fill the day and then disappear when the bell went and we got the bus home. Looking back, I can see how eager I was to be around them all, not just Patrick, all of them, to be admitted into the circle, as though it were an arcane brotherhood that would ease me through the rest of my life if I could only pass the initiation. There was one teacher in particular, an art teacher, who decided that we couldn't sit together because we made too much noise, so he split us up, dotted us across the room. At the time it genuinely felt as though he had transgressed against something sacred. And so we punished him.

We tortured him for the whole term, arguing with everything he said, asking him what the point of sitting around drawing was, demanding to know how it would help us in what we thought of then as our real life. More than once he left the classroom in the middle of the lesson rather than cry in front of us, sending in a different teacher to wrestle back control until the end of the period. The next lesson would roll around, and he would say something about us starting again, having a clean slate. But it never worked, something cruel in us sensed his weakness and we would hurt him over and over again. That memory would be shabby enough on its own, but at the end of term, we did something that still makes me cringe with shame every time the anniversary cycles around.

   I was only saying it to embarrass him, holding my hand up until he gave in and let me speak, shouting across the classroom . . . *sir, we've been horrible to you this term . . . I feel really bad about it . . . Oli is having a birthday party on Saturday, you should come, sir, show us your moves . . . let us say sorry properly.* We were obviously just mocking him. But he came. The man came. Wearing a T-shirt and jeans, the man turned up to a house party full of kids and stood awkwardly in the kitchen asking us about what other subjects we were all studying and a bunch of other painful questions. The moment he got there he must have known it was a joke, that we were laughing at him. But he stayed for an hour, long enough that he could pretend he didn't know what had happened, before putting down his half-drunk bottle of beer and telling us he'd see us all next year. He didn't come back to our school the next year. I can still see him so clearly, leaning against the counter, fingers whitening as he gripped his drink. He was probably younger then than I am now. Fucking hell. Every year I joke with Oli that his birthday is tainted, haunted. But I'm actually not joking at all.

Patrick

I sometimes worry I've stopped learning, stopped paying attention to people. You spend ten hours with the people you love most in the world and you go home not knowing a single new thing about them. Or maybe that isn't true. You see their body move to new music, I suppose. You see them weave in and out of an entirely new crowd of people that you don't know and will probably never speak to. But that's it. It's not much. But it's not nothing, either.

When we were kids, showing off in front of one another, we used to say that we were drinkers, not talkers. But we didn't mean it. Deep down we were hungry to talk but just embarrassed to do it. How many silent ways are there to tell your friends that you love them or that you're scared to lose them or that you're worried you might waste your life? Instead, whenever things had been too quiet for too long, someone would fill the air with something that didn't really matter . . . *Does this cigarette taste weird to you? Can you hear the ring road in the distance? . . . No . . . not now . . . but wait until the wind stops and then listen again.*

By now, that has changed. I think we actually *are* drinkers and not talkers. Eventually the mask becomes the face. Even though it's Oli's birthday, I had made a resolution earlier today to stay off the drugs, because I've started logging in on Sunday mornings to make a bit of money delivering breakfast to people who are hungover enough to pay a four-quid delivery fee for a six-quid meal. It's tiring enough at the best of times, but basically impossible on a comedown. I've tried it before, drinking coffee after coffee after coffee until my actual blood felt like actual coffee. But it made my hands shake and in the end I got too worried about dropping someone's food. I'd tried it with speed too, topping up from the night before, rubbing my gums before each delivery. But it made me erratic on the bike and in the end I got too worried about dropping someone's food. To be honest, I'm not sure I ever signed up for a life in which I am always so worried about dropping other people's food.

The thing is, it's hard not to take drugs when everybody else has taken them and when everybody else also happens to be drinkers and not talkers. So I do. I rack line after line, telling myself I'll stay on the powder and not touch the pills. Until eventually I've taken so much powder that the pills become inevitable. Greed has its own momentum.

I had to do first-aid training when I started my job. I had to pay for it as well, which didn't seem right. But anyway, ever since I did it, I always dose my pills as if I'm a trained doctor, or a research chemist, or one of those academic psychonauts who were allowed to work in universities back in the 1960s. But it doesn't matter, not really. It doesn't matter whether you take your pill whole or whether you take it in quarters three hours apart and try to track what it is doing to you in the meantime. In the end it still feels like your skull has been peeled open a bit and your chest has been peeled open a bit and that maybe your heart has been peeled open a bit as well. And then you piss. And your piss smells sweet and also like chemicals that you don't know the name of.

Four deep in a bar queue that isn't moving, I find myself looking around for Oli. He's the sort of person who compels you to keep an eye on him. I see him dancing between two women, his skinny body all jaunts and angles. I forget that most people in the world don't realise what he used to look like; they just see him now, a bit broken looking, but still a handsome bastard, especially in the spectral gloom of a bar at 2 A.M. One of the women has spilt wine on her leg and it occasionally catches what little light there is. I like it. All three of them look happy. Watching Oli like that makes me wish I could take him away, somewhere less harsh, let him live somewhere near a lake so he can wake up and see water or something. It's too much here. Everything is too much. Oli living here is like watching something extremely bad happen extremely slowly.

Seconds after I finally sit down with a drink I'm pretty sure I won't be able to finish, Conor lumbers over, flops down next to me. He's always been the type to lumber, something heavy in his step. I think about telling him to take a look at Oli, to clock how happy he looks, but he speaks first . . . *did you see that prick? . . . pushed right past me at the bar as if I won't give him a fucking slap.* He's on the turn. It happens. Overall he's steady, but he's always had a mad streak in him, Conor, even back when we said we were drinkers not talkers but weren't really anything of the sort. His first kid is on the way, so the last thing he needs is to be getting into bar fights; Sophie would kill him. And rightly so—heavily pregnant and bailing your boyfriend out of the nick is never ideal. Conor carries bricks for a living, a hoddie. I know he's nervous about the kid but I also know he'll be good at it if he can just keep things together, let the baby soften some of his edges. I don't know Sophie as well, sweet girl, small and pretty, but something distant about her sometimes, didn't grow up here like the rest of us and always seems like she can't wait to fuck off somewhere else. Still, can't be easy living in the shadow of Conor's glower day in, day out, so maybe she's on to something . . . *I swear to god, if he looks over here again* . . . Right, time to go. *Mate, let's just leave it . . . get Oli and we can walk up past the cathedral . . . grab some food . . . get a cab on the hill or walk down to get the night bus.* I know Oli won't want to leave. Why would he? Locked between four bare legs, at least one of which is shiny with spilt wine. But he's coming with us. You can't leave Oli alone. Not worth it. Shiny leg or no shiny leg.

The cathedral is right in the centre of the city. It's lit up from below these days and looks pretty amazing at night even if you don't believe in god, or even if you hate god, or even if you sort of believe in him but don't see why he'd need so many houses. Tonight there are a few foil balloons floating half-heartedly against the brick, abandoned on the way back from a birthday party. The uplights catch the edge of some scaffold that is sticking out of the roof. It makes me think of metal bones which then makes me think of Oli dancing which then makes me look behind to make sure he's still following us. He is. Tapping his phone and swaying from side to side. Conor sees me looking up at the cathedral and tells me that when the scaffold is jutting out like that it means they are repointing the roof . . . *pretty big job, that, repointing.* Talking about buildings seems to help him simmer down.

I can't stand in the kebab shop while Conor and Oli buy food. The sight of all the sweaty, glistening meat is turning my stomach. And the smell. I carry that exact smell so often when I'm delivering. It's supposed to smell like spice and smoke but it smells more like soft fruit gone slightly rotten. There are days I come home and I can smell it on my hair and feel it clinging to the inside of my nose. The idea that other people's food is more appealing than your own is definitely not true if you deliver other people's food for a living.

Just get these two on the night bus without them getting mangled or maimed crossing the road, and then home. I'm already dreading the morning, and already regretting the drugs. I'll sleep on the sofa so I don't wake Shiv or the girls. I won't dream. I never dream when I'm wrecked. It will feel like seconds between the time I pull the blanket over me and the time my alarm goes off. I can't remember the last time I wasn't tired.

Rian

My hotel is close enough that I can walk. Let the cold drain some of the night away. I'm losing my tolerance for such shit clubs, and for such shit drugs. That stuff we were taking tonight made me feel like I was going to start bleeding out of my ears. Minimum requirement: drugs that get the blood pumping, but keep the blood firmly inside your body. I'm fussy about things like that. When I was a kid my old man was always trying to get me to drink milk, wouldn't shut up about the stuff. I'd drink a bit, but never enough to satisfy him, fucking milk nonce that he was . . . *good for the bones . . . good for the bones.* Thing is, I was scared that if I kept drinking milk my bones would grow too big and then eventually burst out of my skin. Everything that is supposed to be inside the body should stay inside the body, that's my rule.

I expected that my hotel would be depressing. And that's exactly how it is. Fifteen minutes' walk out of the centre, which was a promising start. But the room is nowhere near high enough to see the outline of the city, which negates the whole point of getting a hotel outside of the centre to begin with. But it's not all bad. There's a complimentary bottle of wine, something to drink to tip me over into sleep. And flowers. I don't know what they're called, but they're a sort you get all the time in hotels. Purple petals with a sort of inky smudge around the edges. The old man used to have flowers too. One of his passions. Along with the milk. I never used to understand it, but as I get older I'm starting to get what he saw in them.

As a kid, the only flower of his I cared about was the one he had that would only open in the dark. And I only liked that one because sometimes I would get to stay up late and watch it open. Someone near us on the estate had a cat that would come into our garden, eat the flowers and then sick them back up on the flower bed. Insult to injury. But the cat never ate the flower that only opened in the dark. It seemed to know to leave that one alone.

Patrick asked me about the book van tonight, the one that burned down. I had totally forgotten we even had a book van. But I do remember the old library. Maybe when I next see him I'll ask him if he remembers the cat that used to vomit up the flowers, or whether he remembers sleeping over at mine and getting to stay up to watch the night flower open. He'll probably remember. He's more sentimental than me; he keeps the memories in better condition. I'm not sure it's good for the lad, all told.

It's heavy to carry all that around in your head every day. You don't leave enough space for new stuff. Forgetting is massively underrated. It's easier to leave home with an empty bag.

Patrick was always at mine back then. His mom worked late shifts so he'd come back to mine after school. Shiv's mom worked at the same place and she would come back too sometimes. Fucking intense to think those two have kids of their own now. Together. Molly first, who came like a shock, and then in her wake Freya, who by that point seemed inevitable. I suppose it doesn't matter that I can't see the city from my window. I know exactly what it looks like around here. It feels like I've lived here for a thousand years. Like I lived here when it was just mud and disease and people smashing bits of metal with a hammer. I know exactly what it looks like.

Before the hotels, I used to stay with Patrick and Shiv whenever I came back to visit. I liked it at first. It was good to be in that flat with them, on a road I know like the back of my hand. In a home filled with noise, someone always shouting at someone else about something or other. But over time the air had started to shift. Shiv had started apologising for things I couldn't care less about, that their flat was messy or that there wasn't enough hot water. I could feel them fussing over me. So I stopped staying, which I think might have made it worse. I still loved being in that flat though; I envied Patrick his children and his mess and Shiv, always there, looking barely changed since we were teenagers. Same shocking laugh, same birdwing fringe, same red mark on the edge of her jawline.

I remember watching them both playing with their girls and thinking . . . *that's a good thing, that.* They were letting the girls paint the hands of their dolls with red nail varnish because apparently there had been some sort of vicious doll fight during which much blood had been spilled. Barbie dolls, hands dripping with blood. Everybody laughing. And Shiv laughing the most out of all of us. A good thing.

A good thing, but not an easy thing. Always on the edge, those two. Never enough to go around but I still know they wouldn't take a penny from me. I hate to think of it, I hate to think of Patrick filling in all the same fucking forms our parents had to fill in, begging the state for ten quid off your council tax and then getting the form sent back because you used blue ink instead of black. Patrick is always spouting something about the state, about how it should be, about what it should give. I don't get it. All the state ever did for us when we were growing up was watch us and hurt us. I don't know why he thinks it can save him now. He's got the wrong idea.

He doesn't get that there's nothing left. Not here at least. It's nothing, just the middle of the middle, where nothing meets a bit more nothing. If you ask me, he needs to leave. Just attach himself to something that feels good, start there and keep walking. Like I did. Just keep walking. I want to tell him these things, but I know that I won't. I'm already dreading the morning. The sun will come up. Uninvited. Always does.

Patrick

I'm sure at some point in my life I used to wake up smelling like soap and mint. As if the smells had lingered on my skin and my tongue from the night before. Or maybe that's a false memory. But this morning when I wake up everything tastes like putrid iron. Not even as fresh as blood.

The blanket fell off in the night, or I kicked it off in fitful dreams, pedalling a bike in my sleep. It hurts to unfold my legs and stretch them out over the arm of the sofa. I'm too old for the work that I do. Come to think of it, everyone is too old for the work that I do. In a sane world the job wouldn't exist at all. But I suppose there are degrees of shit. And I can say that because I have actually had worse jobs. The type where you turn up, wait around like a prick and then eventually they tell you there isn't any work for you to do after all. As if packing boxes of crisps is some finely calibrated economic science and paying one extra bloke twenty quid is going to topple the whole business deep into the red. Light. Winter sun feels like the brightest sun.

I can hear Shiv in the shower. Up early too. Her soft, wet feet slapping on the lino. I go to her and kiss between her shoulders. She tastes of soap. That's more like it. She is hugging her knees to her chest and painting her toes where bits of the polish have flaked away. Shiv still tears me apart after all of these years. I've spent my life loving her. In the very truest sense, I had nothing better to do. She has a tattoo of an artichoke running up the outside of her thigh, which I hated for about an hour after she got it but which now I absolutely adore. I can still picture it so clearly, her smirk when I asked her why the hell she'd got a vegetable drawn on her leg. A vegetable that only rich idiots eat . . . *because artichokes are plants with flesh . . . because they are flowers with claws. Because they have a heart and the heart is furry and the heart looks like a pussy . . . and you can eat it but it fights back. Because an artichoke is an odd creature . . . and because they taste good . . . you just haven't tried them.*

Another kiss and then out. Suck in the cold air. It's my favourite part of the job, the ride into the city, no orders yet, catching snatches of songs coming out of car windows and shops as I pass them, or playing songs in my earphones that I chose while I drank my morning coffee. I don't really mind which. There were a few times when I thought I'd predicted what song I was going to hear next. Like I'd think of a particular song and be humming it and then a few seconds later I'd cycle past a shop and hear it playing. When I first told Shiv that she laughed and said I had probably just already heard it in the air without noticing, being played on one of the handful of radio stations that still existed. She was probably right. But it was less romantic that way. The same thing happened when we were kids, first falling in love. I told her I was born lucky because I'd never seen a star on its own, only ever in a pair or a cluster. And she told me I'd got stars confused with magpies. You get thoughts and memories like that all the time when you're riding. The faster you pedal, the faster they come. *Turn left . . . are brochures still a thing? Are they still made of that glossy paper that sticks to the roof of your mouth? Turn left again . . . how come some people still look pale even when they are blushing?*

On the final stretch into town, I pass Oli on the road, but he doesn't see me when I lift my arm and wave to him. Not sure where he's headed, but he looks purposeful, a little bounce to him, as though something of the night before has lingered. The leg that was shiny with wine, maybe. Slick in the memory . . . *turn right in two hundred metres.* It's nice to think of

Oli getting clean; I wonder if he ever will be. I imagine hugging him and him smelling the way paper smells when it comes out of the photocopier. And his mind like paper too, dry, with clean edges and plenty of space for words . . . *you have reached your destination.* He's tried it before though, and nothing got drier, everything got more wet and more swampy until one morning Rian and I found him folded up on his bedroom floor, sweating, with his duvet pressed against his chest. But this morning he looked good. Maybe it's the light. Winter sun always feels like the brightest sun.

It's not just Oli. Most people don't see me when I wave to them from my bike. When I first started I thought they were pretending not to notice, because they were embarrassed of me. Or worse, because they were embarrassed *for* me. More likely it's just that I pass them fairly quickly and everyone who delivers food has to wear identical jackets. Overdesigned and garish, but identical. The worst of both worlds. Add in the regulation black helmet and the regulation black face mask that is supposed to stop the pollution from killing you long enough to finish your shift, and there isn't much of a face left to notice.

On my first drop of the day I pick up a brown bag full of fried breakfast food and a tray of elaborate coffee that I know will spill on the journey, something that I am powerless to prevent. Up the hill to the slightly nicer bit of town. I saw one of the other delivery riders fall off his bike on this hill once. It was fucking horrible. Happens a lot though. The quicker you ride the more money you make, so people make stupid mistakes. I can remember him pretending he wasn't hurt, hobbling back to his bike, gingerly, all bandy legged. Riding off. And then stopping again to make sure the food in his bag wasn't ruined. Remembering it turns last night's drink and drugs sour in my stomach. I can smell the oil coming from the brown bag.

Doorbell. Here you go mate. I'm here in my face mask and my helmet and my stupid jacket to hand deliver you a load of things that I myself have precisely none of. Like time. And breakfast. No cash for a tip. Don't worry about it. You can do it on the app later if you want. Which you won't. Always the way: the days start with sucking in the cold air and the quick memories and questions that come with it. Sharp. But they don't end sharp. They end like a blurred photo. Not an arty one made with a filter. The type of blurred that used to make the old man angry when he picked up his pictures from the developers at the back of the chemist. The days end with you wanting to make everything solid again, maybe plant things, buy bags of gravel, peel a banana, cut a cold apple with a knife.

Rian

It's a good morning, on the back of a fairly average night. Slightly perverse, but these days I'm starting to enjoy the morning after more than the night before. The slowness, the thickness in your head and in your mouth, the excuse for not doing much of anything. I'm sick of there always being something to do. Slow. Slow cigarette out of the window; I'll pay the fine if I have to. Slow coffee, which I'll abandon halfway through. Slow wank, listening to the sound of high heels moving through the corridor and on the street below my window. And ice. I fucking love ice. Get the texture right and I honestly think ice might be my favourite food. Money doesn't buy you happiness, apparently. But it does buy you pretty much unlimited access to ice, whenever you want it. Get rich, eat ice. I should make an effort to remember that. Whenever it all seems a bit much, think of the ice.

I said to Patrick last night that I'd try to pop over after he had finished his shift, see Shiv and the girls before I leave. But I'm not sure I can. Something doesn't feel quite right, like a lash in your eye that you know is there but can't see even when you look in the mirror and pull your cheek down like a ghoul. I seemed off last night, awkward, older maybe. Unused to the rhythm of the talking and the thinking. Out of practice. I keep thinking about the heavy silver jewellery my old man used to wear, half of it punched with those Irish knots you see on Dublin tourist tat. That's how the thought of being home has started to feel, knotted and metallic. Doesn't matter how long I look at the shape, I can't find a way to unpick the knot. I send Shiv a text.

Patrick will be out on his bike, and anyway, he'd be more likely to try to change my mind. *Really sorry . . . don't think I'll be able to make it round today. Work is a bit mad, and I should head back. Gutted to miss you and the girls, give them a kiss from me . . .* Reading her reply, I can't shake the feeling she doesn't believe me. But then again, I always feel that way when I'm lying. *Ah, that's a shame . . . we were all looking forward to seeing you. Never mind. See you soon . . . and the kids send their love, you know they are crazy about you.*

And I was crazy about them right back. It was one of the best feelings in the world to sit there and answer their kid questions while they clambered all over me. *Why is your hair black but Dad's hair is brown? Do you live in a house as well? Do you have a dog? A rabbit? Why does your face smell of flowers?* Fuck me. Such great kids. I still remember the night we celebrated Molly being born. A baby. Unimaginable a year before. Not yet knowing there would be another one the next year, and that by then it would feel like the most normal thing in the world. We felt like kids ourselves, Patrick the only one with any worries, fussing about leaving Shiv on her own with the baby for the first time. One of those long, light summer nights. We had got all ambitious for the special occasion and decided to drive out into the countryside, with no real plan to speak of, other than to get drunk next to a tree instead of next to a car park.

We were lively that day, full with that special type of happiness that comes when you know that things are ending and things are beginning, all at the same time. Conor was there, on lighter form for a change, singing at the top of his voice, clapping his hands and trying to get everyone in the car to sing along as well. Took about ten seconds before we were all at it. Hitting the steering wheel and the headrest and the dashboard in time with the music. Conor had quite a nice singing voice, but it was quickly drowned out by all of us bashing things and chanting the words as loudly as we could. I think we managed about two minutes before we all collapsed into laughter. For the rest of the night, you'd hear one of us humming the melody under our breath, like it had got stuck in all of our throats and we couldn't manage to hack it up.

The less I come home, the more I've started to send Patrick and Shiv gifts. It is a shit, cowardly habit, and I know it has to stop. I hate doing it, and I think they hate it too. I've stopped knowing what they like or what they would want in their flat. A few times when I've been round, I can see they've put the stuff I've given them somewhere prominent, just so I can see that they use it or like it or whatever. It's horrible. The worst was a few years back when I got Patrick some shoes for his birthday. They were the same type I'd bought myself after I closed my first big deal, but they looked really stupid on him. They didn't match any of his clothes, and when he wore them on a night out, Conor and Oli and the rest of the lads took the piss out of him. Told him he looked like a fugitive who'd stole someone else's shoes. He laughed along. But I didn't. I was mortified. Who buys their friend a pair of shoes? What a prick.

There are days when I think I should just stop coming back altogether. Just cut the guide rope. But I can't leave it be. When I have nowhere else to go, I come here. Here is where I come to find things. Stepping off the train and seeing the old streets, the building where the community centre used to be, it's like finding a wallet on the street, opening it and seeing a driving licence with your own face on it. Lost things. My old man was always losing things, always walking around with a fire at his back, wondering where things had disappeared to.

There was a stage when I hated him. Everything seemed to be getting harder and more messed up and I was angry that he wasn't trying to fix anything. It was as if the house was only ever a few minutes from going up in flames, but he wasn't bothered because he quite liked the smell of smoke. For a while, our life seemed like an electrical wire hanging a few inches above a puddle, harmless for now, but only for now. He died a few years back, only in his late fifties. Too early, but not that unusual, not when you spend your life breaking your body mixing cement and then drinking at night to dull the pain in your arms and back.

For the last few years of his life, he barely spoke. Most of all I remember him having this strange quality, where whatever material he was touching would sort of enter his body, via his hands and his veins and then eventually up his neck and into his face. If he was at the kitchen table it would be as though he was made of hard, old wood, but if he was at the sink, near the metal, he'd be colder and flatter and more cruel. I'd try to speak to him in the morning, when he was still in bed, softer, or outside where there was plenty of air and light. It didn't seem weird when he died; it just washed over me. It makes me feel a bit ashamed.

But we were always the type of family who kept the dead close. Everyone believed in ghosts, people were always spending Saturday nights seeing mediums and psychics in the back room of pubs, people were always telling you that if you didn't put your coat on you'd catch your death. It seemed like every adult in the family had a story about how their kids almost came into the world as dead as a stone, with a cord wrapped around their neck, and that every teenager in the family had a story about someone who wasn't coming back to school because their mom had found them slung up over the summer holidays, also with a cord wrapped around their neck. Like a grim callback to a bad joke.

I'm crazy about them too, Shiv . . . send me an up-to-date picture when you get a sec. R xx

Conor

Some people have a talent for being young. Oli had that, a local celebrity, lighting up classrooms. I didn't. My only talent was violence. I was good at violence, and it was useful when we were kids. One of those things though, like being able to drink a lot, a superpower for a while and then a poison before you know it. The first real fight, stretching to reach his school shirt from across the table, and then the blankness. Coming to and feeling my mouth full of blood, iron and viscous, swallowing it down and being surprised that it tasted O.K. And then the face of the kid, the shock of it. His face was black with blood. Slick. I remember thinking there was too much blood, that it must be coming from somewhere else other than his body. Once the adrenaline had worn off, something else rose in me to take its place. Something like pride, a sort of low-level buzz I carried around in my back pocket for weeks. The next time I had the chance, I did it again, and before long I wasn't waiting for an excuse, I was making it happen whenever I needed the feeling back.

It's mostly under control now. It might slip out once a year if I've been drinking too much and somebody presses my buttons, but on the whole, it stays buried. Or at least it has done until recently. Since Sophie has been pregnant, I've felt something rising again, mostly only in my dreams but occasionally it leaks into the daylight as well. The more her body swells, the more I can feel it. As if the more new life there is, the more the darkness grows. Lately I've been having the bleakest dreams, picking through piles of ash in search of a shard of white bone that I'm convinced I need to salvage. Or worse, visions of Sophie hurting the baby. A recurring one of me walking into the bedroom and seeing her wide eyed, spit foaming in the corners of her mouth, swinging the baby headfirst into the wall. I always wake before I can get to her and stop it. I think Sophie can sense it too. The closer we get to the baby arriving, the more distant she is becoming. Colder, more wary, scared even, as if being near me might pull her and the baby towards something awful. She doesn't need to feel like that though, I'll sort it out, like I have done before. And anyway, I'm making changes, I've got plans.

I know I'm a lucky bastard and I won't ruin it by letting us get stuck in a fucking rut like most people around here. The others have never really liked Sophie, I don't think, even though Shiv and Patrick have always made an effort with her.

But they don't know how hard I am to love, how knotted up I was for years before I met her. Things aren't as easy between us as I'd like, but I still have a clear picture of Sophie when we first met: tiny, a bit flinty maybe, but with just enough love to open me up and unpick me. Any more would have been more than I could manage. And we can find our way back to that, the two of us, the three of us even, I know we can. I've got an idea that will protect us, take care of us.

Because Rian has it right. You can't just wait around and expect things to change. Or at least not to change for the better. In my experience things are either gradually getting worse, or they get worse all of a sudden and then you realise they've been rotting away without you even noticing. Take the Meadows. The retirement home on the edge of the estate. When we were kids, we were petrified by it, used to dare each other to climb the fence and look into the window. You'd sometimes hear shouting and moaning from in there, or see a face pressed against the glass, watching the traffic, or waiting for a visitor. It always seemed a fucking horrible place. The type of place where there was only ever light by accident. Fast forward ten years though, and I'd stopped finding it scary, I'd stopped noticing it at all. It was just the Meadows, the place I had to walk past on my way to work every morning. And then one day it was gone. Knocked down over a weekend and the plot has been empty ever since. That seemed scarier to me than the moaning and the faces at the window ever did. Where did all the residents go? Had it been empty for years and I just hadn't noticed?

 We got up the nerve, or the stupidity, to try to break in there once, Oli, Rian and me. We must have been about fourteen, and I think we had the bright idea of trying to steal some computers and then selling them at one of the exchange shops in town that never asked any questions about what you took in. The alarm went off as soon as we got near the front door and we ran away, laughing. Out of nervousness at first, and then properly laughing when we were sure we were far enough away to be safe. We made a pact not to tell Patrick what we had done. Rian insisted on it. He always cared what Patrick thought of him, even back then. He was right though, Patrick wouldn't have liked it, wouldn't have seen the funny side. He was always going on about how it was all right to nick things from the supermarket but never from the corner shop, that sort of thing. I used to think he'd end up as one of those town councillor types, arguing on Tuesday nights about funding for the primary school or how to get better recycling bins or whatever. I imagined people seeing him on the telly and calling him a wanker... *who does he think he is?* And all of us who knew him saying things like... *leave him be... yeah, we went to school with him... trust me, he's one of us... he used to write on his trainers in biro just like the rest of us... decent footballer as well, but yeah, I get it... fair point, he does look a bit of a dickhead in that suit.*

 Can't just wait around. I hardly see anyone other than Oli

and Patrick these days anyway, usually only when we've got an excuse to get fucked up. And even that might stop soon. Oli is a mess, Patrick never has the money; we'll end up like everyone else we know, closed doors, drinking in front of the telly until we fall asleep and saying things like . . . *me? . . . just had a quiet one . . . you?* to each other on a loop until the end of time. I've got a kid on the way; something had to be done. That's why I asked Rian for the money the other night. He was probably quite pissed, but he said he'd do it. A few hundred thousand up front, and I could build ten flats where the Meadows used to be. With the people I know, I could do them cheap enough that we make ten times that amount on the backend. If there's one thing I know about, it's buildings. And I can't carry bricks for ever, not with a kid on the way. Rian gets that. He'll win out of it too; he knows I wouldn't let him down.

And I'm sure people will buy them. It's easy to think about the estate as a total dead end, but it's not. If you watch carefully, you can already feel that people are starting to come, the younger ones we knew from school and who can't face it at their parents' any more, a few who went to the college in the centre and then decided to stick around, even the odd few with money who get on the train every day to their cushy office jobs and are looking for a bargain. Who else is paying Patrick four quid a pop to deliver them burgers? Sophie would rather we just left entirely, just went somewhere else before the baby was born. She doesn't see the place like I do, doesn't remember when it was better than it is now.

There are nights when I rub slippery oil on the silver stretch marks spreading across her stomach and tell her that things will be fine. And nights when I twist her hair up against the back of her head so I can kiss her shoulders and neck and tell her things will be fine. But there are some days that I don't tell her about at all. Like the day when I started panicking because I thought the packet of minced beef in the fridge looked like maggots, or the leftovers of an industrial accident, and I ended up retching and throwing it in the bin even though we couldn't afford the waste. I also don't tell her that sometimes I don't trust the waterline on the kettle, so I have to keep opening it to check that there's enough liquid in there to make the tea. And how when the water is almost boiled I get freaked out by the way the kettle shakes and moves on the surface and have to turn it off before it's finished. And how then I worry that the tea won't be hot enough. I always get the colour right though. The same way Sophie has always liked it. *Paper-bag brown.* When she doesn't say anything about the temperature I start to think everything will be fine again. And so that's what I tell her . . . *everything will be fine.*

Oli

I've started to hate the way they all look at me. As if they pity me. They don't think that I notice, but I do. They've got no reason to pity me, I'm no sadder than the rest of them. In fact, I might even be less sad, because at least I'm high. Sad and high has got to be better than just sad. Even the other night, on my own birthday, I could feel their eyes on me, checking up, making sure I wasn't doing anything stupid. Thing is, I was doing something stupid, we were all doing something stupid; that was the whole point of going out in the first place, to do stupid things. Except apparently I'm the exception, the special case. Well, fuck that.

Anyway, they think I'm worse than I am. If they saw some of the people I sell to, they'd realise what messed up really looks like. You can see them progress over time. Six months or so and their skin starts to go white, another six months and it starts to look see-through and then after a couple of years they get that weird blue glow, like they've got strip lights running along their jawbones. I'm nowhere near that far gone and I don't intend to ever get there, either. I only use to shape the day, blur the edges a bit. Nobody tells you this, but if you're comfortable strapping a belt around your arm, you can choose how fast the time goes, how fast the hours are swallowed up. Imagine being able to press fast forward on your own life, six hours at a time. That's what it's like. Useful. It makes the small things more interesting too, which, trust me, is a serious bonus if your life is entirely boring and made up entirely of small things. Makes me bloody love my fridge, for example. I'll stand there for minutes, not sure what I like the most, the artificial light, the cold or the humming. But happy all the same.

Or the TV. Brown makes you love the TV. The glow. I like the wildlife programmes the best. The type where a massive, deadly animal chases down a slightly less massive and slightly less deadly animal, which luckily happens to be slightly faster than the thing it is being chased by. I like the bits when an animal finally gets caught and you watch it surrender, spilling its entrails and stomach acid all over the grass. Those bits always feel like a relief. But I also like the parts when you end up changing your mind about which animal you are rooting for. Sometimes the hunted animal will find some of its family and they all turn on the predator together. When that happens I switch my allegiance straight away; I'm not in the business of forming strong attachments. But the best episode I ever saw was about seals. The seals just sat there on the ice, eating fish and sliding around a bit, and then out of nowhere a fucking polar bear just crashed up through the ice, killing as many seals as it could, pushing its teeth right into their necks. I loved that episode. I wasn't sad for the seals. It was nice to think you could have a life like that, eating fish and sliding around, and then be dead before you know it, no worrying, no slow decline, gone before you'd even finished chewing.

I'm the only one who sees things properly around here; I'm the only one who knows the roads and the streets and the air properly. The way the branches fracture the sky. I know this place like the back of my hand. And the front of my hand. If there were ancient rivers running under this estate, I reckon I could probably find them using a couple of sticks. At least I pay attention. At least I see things properly. They all act like I should already be in the ground, like I'm already rotting away. But I'm not the one who's rotting. They should have seen me the morning after my birthday, out walking before the sun came up, miles of flat, dry roads edging their way in every direction. On good days, days like that, the roads feel like veins, or like roots, pulling in life and sending some back out in return. They don't see that. They don't see those mornings when instead of a sunrise, the air just seems to change colour, getting pinker and pinker until before you know it there is proper light and the pink has gone. I walk miles sometimes, while the rest of them are still asleep. I was walking the morning after my birthday. I thought I saw Patrick on his bike. Might not have been him, they make all those poor bastards dress exactly the same. But I raised my hand just in case.

I know they mean well, but I've started to worry they have forgotten what I used to be like, what I used to need, what I still need. Like the other night, with Patrick and Conor pulling me away from those women and making me leave with them instead. It might have been nice to end my birthday in bed with a woman, surely they get that? Instead, I went home imagining it. What it might be like to feel our hips banging together while we fucked, or what it might have felt like to have her pull me closer while I came, or Jesus, just the smell of someone new in the room, breath like sweet cold milk or something. They take care of me, but I don't just want the practical stuff. Conor offers me bits of work, but I can't handle the hours and it's easier to make my money selling. And Rian tells me for hours on end that my dealing skills are transferable. Fucking transferable. The twat. I don't just want the practical stuff; I want the good stuff of life too.

The meat of it. It's all I've ever wanted. The meat of it. Even when I was a kid. My mom was mad on the Bible, and because she was mad on the Bible, we all had to be mad on the Bible as well. Not sure I've ever read another book, but I know that one back to front. There's that bit when Jesus writes on the ground with a stick, but we are never told what he writes. Only time in the whole book the lad writes anything and we don't know what it is. I needed to know what he wrote. Mom didn't know. Nobody knew. I was sure that if we could just find out, then that would be it, that would be the meat of things. On the bad days, when I don't feel connected to anything, when nothing seems real, I still think about that. What did he write?

SHIV

Left arm out, and there's space. Right arm out, and there's space. The first few seconds of realising Patrick is not in our bed are always horrible, but after that, I take the chance to spread out a bit, make some weird shapes, maybe even roll over once or twice. Space is at a premium here, same as quiet. I take it where I can get it. Snatch at it like I'm hungry. Our room is the smallest room in a small flat; Molly and Freya share the larger one, the year between them already beginning to show, tastes and habits starting to form and clash. Because our room is small, I keep it clean. I can't sleep if there's mess in the bedroom. Especially if it is mess caused by things that should never have been in the bedroom in the first place. Clothes or whatever are bad enough, but sometimes I come in here and Patrick has left plates, or shampoo, or unopened letters. Not having that. Crosses a line.

He'll be on the sofa, which means he's decided to do an early shift. The morning after a night out, as well. He's a good man. He's quieter these days; I know things are wearing on him, that he feels ashamed of the work he does, that he should have made different choices. I keep telling him that it's O.K. to be angry, nobody should have to practically kill themselves to barely keep food on the table, but that he should never be ashamed. Maybe he could have made different choices, but so what, we all could have. Temporary solutions end up becoming the substance of your life. That's what life is: something permanent made up of loads of temporary solutions.

I should shower. If the girls are still asleep Patrick will do what he normally does, come in while I'm drying myself and slide his hands around my waist, kiss me good morning. There are days when I hate it, when I don't have time for it, when the last thing I want is to be pawed at while I'm trying to brush my fucking teeth. But I try to remember that deep down it's a good thing he's still like that after all this time. Not bad going. Fifteen years, on and off, and we are still solid. I can remember scratching P+S on a bus stop when we were just kids, and Patrick saying something he thought was clever like . . . *that looks like the world's most basic algebra equation.* Always the smart-arse. When I first found out I was pregnant, still a kid myself in some ways, I told him I was scared and that under no circumstances should he start making any of his so-called fucking witty comments about it. He promised. A promise that lasted about three hours. But I was glad when the jokes came. That was when I knew we'd be alright.

Text from Rian says he isn't coming round today after all. Says something has come up at work. I lose track of what his work even is these days, so I suppose that could be true. Or maybe he's just too wrecked from last night to make the journey. I hope it's not anything else. The last couple of times he's been here things haven't felt quite the same as they used to, a bit more awkward maybe, like the words weren't coming as easily. I worry that things might be fracturing a bit between the rest of them and Rian, coming apart so slowly that you barely notice until something breaks. I've known them all since I was a kid—Oli, Conor, Rian—but I've never really been on the inside, not quite. They'd disagree with that, but they'd be wrong. It's like they have a private language. If something that consists mostly of silence can be called a language, which I suppose it can. If you didn't know them, I swear to god you'd think they hated each other, sitting there barely speaking. But it's not like that. Born in the same hospital, growing up basically next door. Sit with them long enough and you get the impression they came out of the womb muttering to each other. The girls will be gutted about Rian not coming; they love having him around. So do I, to be honest. It's good to have new energy in the flat. Something from the outside.

New energy matters. Maybe not as much as it used to, but it still matters. A lifetime ago, before the girls were born, I even occasionally sought it out. When Patrick and I had off periods, when we were figuring out if it was the stupidest thing in the world to spend your life with the very first person you fell for. Nothing came of any of it, thank god, but it does cross my mind every now and then, how free I felt back then. Surely that's normal. We all think about the hundred different ways our life could have happened. It would be weird not to. You imagine what it might feel like to have a different body on top of you, a different voice in your ear. And to live in a different world. A house big enough that you didn't have to drive yourself mad keeping it tidy, one of those baths that fills with water if you clap twice, a garden spilling out from your back door.

The day passes gently enough, and then the storm. Always the storm. Paper and crayons all over the table to keep the girls busy while I cook them dinner. Two mousy heads, bowed in concentration, ready to erupt into argument, uneasy peace. Too early for me to eat but I'll eat with them anyway. Dirty pots in scalding water, the distracting light of the TV for an hour, the screams of protest when it's time for a bath. The I don't want to and the I'm not tired. And then the calm.

I've already got wine in, so I invite Sophie round to help me drink it. She's allowed a glass or two, so she can do her bit for the cause. Text Patrick to say that Rian isn't coming so if he wants to work a double shift he can. I like Sophie; I can't say she's riveting company, but I like her. But two hours in, I regret it. She's smashed off two glasses, and refusing to switch over to Diet Coke even though she's pregnant. Whatever, her choice. But she won't stop talking about how Conor is going to ruin them with some stupid scheme to build new flats, how he's borrowing money left right and centre and trusting the wrong people . . . *Seriously, Shiv, the people he works with are dickheads . . . useless . . . and to be honest he's not much better . . . always on edge . . . he's not nice to be around at the minute.* She'd rather just leave, go and live somewhere closer to her parents before the baby is born. I feel for her, but although I'm not proud of it, I'm bored. I tell her we are out of wine even though there are still two more bottles in the cupboard. I go to bed early, just drunk enough not to feel guilty for cutting Sophie short and sending her home even though I could tell she needed to talk.

Later that night I feel Patrick climb into bed, trying not to wake me. Half asleep I tell him to talk to me . . . *tell me some things . . . tell me some things that aren't important . . . tell me some things that I don't have to remember.*

Rian

There's always that point on the train journey when you notice the buildings change. At first there is nothing much at all, and then after half an hour or so the nothing much starts to give way to the industrial estates and storage units scattered on the cheap land that rings the city. Another half an hour and you hit the brick. Clusters of houses in dark red and wet brown. They are probably villages, but I've never really known what the difference is between a village and a town. Something to do with council tax boundaries maybe. And then finally, the glass. The closer you get to where the money is, the more glass you see. There's that idea that you can tell what a society values most by which are its tallest buildings. First it was the churches, then the town halls and the courthouses, and now it's the glass: the banks and the insurance firms, top to bottom glass, with a view of the river that splits the city in two.

Tired in my fucking bones. And too young to be saying things like tired in my fucking bones. I don't think going back to visit is helping, being around it all, being the only one who clocks that things are getting worse back there. It's exhausting. The rest of them can't see it, their faces are pressed too close to the picture to notice the details changing. There won't be any new work; in six months there won't even be as much work as there is now. Give it a year and everyone there will be delivering food to the people who have moved nearby because the houses are dirt cheap and it's close enough to the train station to be bearable. Patrick is a canary in the coalmine. Ghost of Christmas future. Always was ahead of the game.

The only one with half a clue is Conor. He can see there might be some money to be made on new flats, and he's probably right, there usually is. Unless you invested in the Gaza Strip or Central Syria, parking a bit of money in basic housing over the last decade has generally worked out pretty well. People need places to live, the government won't build, and there is only so much land. Supply and demand. Patrick would hate me for saying that, but that's the reality. We all watched that tower block on the news: people like us burning to death in their sleep or throwing babies out of windows hoping something would break the fall. How could you see that and still pretend that anyone gave a fuck about us? Get as angry as you like, but as far as I can tell, either we do it ourselves or it just doesn't get done. Those are the choices. Anyway, I said I'd lend Conor the money, and I was pleased he asked. If he can genuinely get the flats done as cheaply as he said, then there will be plenty left for me to pick up on the backend and plenty for him as well. Piece of piss making money when you already have money. Harder to lose it. Stick it in assets, let the base grow and live off the yields. Passive income, they call it. Extremely passive income, if you ask me. Doing absolutely fuck all income, more like.

Off the train and into the flow of the city, into the shuffling and the sighing and the speed. The buses I'll never catch, remembrance gardens for wars I don't know anything about, shops selling expensive watches which hardly seem to have any watches in them, cleaners moving from building to building while everyone else is asleep, buggies stuffed with well-dressed kids, old lads in nice suits, newsagents that never seem to close. Millions of people moving through the streets the way insects move through rain, by instinct, never letting a drop hit their wings or slow them down. Keep moving. Keep moving until the wave of it all washes me up at the front door of my flat. The sound of my keys as they land on the kitchen table, the feeling that I'm O.K. here, that this is not the sort of place where lives get worse. I can see a cathedral from my window, bigger than the one back home, but tiny from the perspective of the twenty-seventh floor. As if I could reach right out of the window, touch the roof of the cathedral and then slam the spire straight through my palm. That's how small it looks from up here. I feel O.K. here. This is not the sort of place where lives get worse.

I message Emma, tell her I've come back a day earlier than I planned, that I'm free tonight if she wants to come round. I didn't tell Patrick about her while I was back, and I don't really know why. I've been seeing her for a few months now and if I leave it much longer without introducing her, or at least mentioning her, it will start to seem weird. It just never came up. There wasn't the right moment. I'll do it soon though, before things get too serious.

The first thing you'll notice about Emma is that she is stunning. I don't think I've ever seen anyone who looks like her before. Her face seems to be made up of new angles, as if nobody had thought to make a face like that until she came along. Long back, small, round shoulders, quick to laugh, quick to make me laugh. It's good. It's a good thing. In an hour, she'll be here, and we can talk and fuck and shower together and before the end of the night I won't have to think too much about Patrick on his bike, or how I lied to Shiv about having to head back, or about how pissed off Oli looked when they dragged him home while he was dancing. In an hour she'll be here. Cold vodka in a clear glass. Clear ice. A clear window to a clear sky. A river and a spire that could slip right through my skin.

Two

Patrick

When the text comes, the summons, it has been almost a year since I last saw Rian. Probably the longest I've gone without seeing him since we were kids. The last time he was here, he was supposed to come over the morning after Oli's birthday, but he messaged Shiv while I was at work saying something had come up. Fair enough. I remember Shiv texting me that day and saying not to bother rushing home, that I could work a back-to-back shift if I wanted. I didn't want to, obviously, but I did it anyway.

Almost a whole year since that night. He seems to have stopped sending gifts, which is a fucking relief. And I know he's doing O.K. because he called the other day while I was on the bike, left a voicemail because I couldn't answer. Met a girl apparently. About time. And now he's texted us to come to the city to meet her.

At some point since we last saw Rian, new people moved into the flat next door. They moved in so quickly I didn't even notice it happen. But once they were there, you could really feel it, flats in this block are all the same: two bedrooms, low ceilings, thin walls, uncomfortable proximity. The flat next door had been empty for at least a year and then overnight it was leaking noise and life right into our home. Their music was loud, and constant. Mostly, I quite like it, perks things up a bit, but on nights when I sleep on the sofa and it keeps me awake, I start to hear it as an incessant, violent throb. There's absolutely no way I'm going to become one of those people who moan about people playing their music too loud, though. Absolutely not. That's waltzing in the graveyard behaviour. And I hear them fucking sometimes. He has one of those voices that seems to slide through brickwork as if it doesn't exist. I'm not going to complain about that, either. Can you imagine? *Morning mate, sorry to bother you . . . it's just that sometimes it feels like you're literally shouting in my ear about how hard your cock is . . . cheers.* I thought that flat would stay empty for ever, if I'm honest. I can understand why someone who grew up here might decide not to leave, once their roots had got all tangled in the mud. But I can't really get my head around the idea of people coming here from somewhere else entirely, to put down a whole new set of roots. But maybe Conor is right. Maybe new people will keep coming.

Hard to imagine, though. I've lived in the block my whole life, and then had the council tenancy handed down to me like a family heirloom. Change was a rare thing. The flat on the other side of us has had the same people in it since before I was born. No new roots there. Just a sign in the window that says *Jesus is coming, be ready.* The sign is badly faded from decades of sun, or maybe by the light of the Lord himself, who knows? I only know what it says for sure because I remember it from before the letters were bleached to oblivion. All we ever hear from that side is their TV, turned up so loud that the sound periodically distorts. Adverts and news. Then more adverts and more news. *Buy this piece of utterly useless shit . . . there is probably going to be a war . . . oh, and buy this useless piece of shit as well . . . the planet is basically on fire.* That sort of thing, on an endless loop. Still, there are days when I find it moving, the rhythm of a life spent together like that. I imagine them as companionable, and in love, passing each other tissues and glasses of water and wondering what they might have for dinner even though they know full well what they will end up having for dinner. I'm sentimental though, because for all I know they might hate each other. They might use the incredibly loud television to drown out the monotonous whine of one another's voice lest they be driven to slowly strangle each other to death with their weak, elderly hands. I doubt it though; they always smile at us, and push a card through the door at Christmas.

Shiv says that I'm getting too thin and I'm starting to agree. I liked it at first but now my clothes are too big and I don't want to have to buy new ones. And when I look in the mirror I've started to worry that I look the way my old man looked when he took a temp job as a postman and developed the physique of a crack addict who runs ultra-marathons for fun. It's hard though. If you carry other people's food around all day then practically all food starts to seem unappealing. And I don't really have a boss to get angry at, other than my phone, the green dot on the map and the timer in the corner. So in a weird way, I've started to blame the food. If the food wasn't there, frying in cafes, spinning on spits, slopping around in oversized pots, then I wouldn't have to spend my life ferrying it about to people who wanted it. I know that sounds insane, but I've started to hate the food. It's as if I'm a horse and the box of chicken nuggets in my bag is my master. A master who might reach over and whip me, just for a bit of fun, just to break up his day.

Some perks of this job: you get to know the moon really well, and sometimes the air is so cold it feels like you have grown a new pair of lungs. *Some drawbacks of this job*: there is no light at the end of this tunnel, there is nothing undiscovered or new or untamed, or dazzling.

And you end up looking skinny and awful from riding a bike all day. Oh, and also you end up imagining that you are a horse being whipped by a box of cruel chicken nuggets.

Rian

I met Emma the way all people with money meet their partners. Other rich people introduced us. It seems to be an unwritten rule: you feel people starting to hover around you at parties and telling you about someone or other that you just *have* to meet. The longer I went on attending things on my own, the more intense the hovering got. There was something upsetting to them about the fact that I hadn't immediately taken the opportunity to permanently anchor myself to their world. Wealth can't be untethered or it might drift away, might slip out of the city one night and spend itself somewhere else. Patrick would say they were *reproducing their class composition* or something, but to me it just felt like a type of creepy eugenics.

But still, I yielded. And I'm glad that I did. I couldn't have carried on much longer the way I was living. It was undignified.

I might well have ended up dying of shame. I'd got into a bad habit of drinking on my own, looking out my window and over the city, listening to the sound of the traffic and the muffle of the river. Sometimes I would get drunk enough that I would leave the flat and follow the lights and the taxis until I found a bar that looked promising. I'd sit there on my own, down drink after drink, scrolling on my phone or picking at coasters, fanning them, stacking them and unstacking them. Some nights I would find myself clicking through pictures of people I used to go to school with, girls I'd kissed or fucked as a teenager, or girls I was desperate to kiss or fuck as a teenager but who never let me touch them. A pathetic urge to nudge them, draw attention to myself, show them that I had moved on, made something of myself, whatever that meant. Most of them just looked so old, so beaten. We probably all did, but you just don't notice it as clearly with people you see more often. There were some real extremes though. Conor used to talk about the baby–tooth equation, that each baby they had seemed to cost them another tooth. It was cruel, but he had a point.

Nights like that, I wouldn't realise how fucked I was until I stood up, or until I tried to pay my bill and ended up just mashing the keypad of the card machine with my fingers. Walk home to sober up, tracing the bend of the water and stopping every few minutes to steady myself against a wall or a car that looked old enough not to have an alarm. I'd order food on the walk so it would get to my flat at the same time as me. Mounds of fried chicken and pizza, most of which I wouldn't eat, or that I'd throw up in the morning as I tried to fight my hangover. I'd give the riders ridiculous tips, twice what I paid for the food. But it didn't make me feel any better about doing it.

There were other women before Emma. Sort of. Sometimes I would fuck strangers, but I'd always want them to leave straight afterwards. Or if I had no polite way of getting them out, I'd end up not sleeping, feeling strange about them being there in the darkness, making tiny animal sounds. They would close their eyes and it would bother me that I didn't know what colour they were under the eyelids. I paid for sex as well. Not often, but maybe ten times before I met Emma. I would order an escort to my flat the same way I'd order food, tapping the requirements into an app and then waiting on high alert for the doorbell. When I paid it was normally fine, except with the ones who were particularly good at their job, particularly concerned that I enjoyed myself, and that I got exactly what I wanted. Because the trouble was I never really knew what I wanted. The finding out was the fun thing, but that type of meandering wasn't really on the cards when you paid by the hour.

Apart from that, there were a few who stuck around for a bit longer. A month or so each for the sarcastic, sceptical graduate student with the hair under her arms, and for the divorced friend of a friend who once stopped mid-conversation and asked me why I had never bought her shoes. And about ten weeks for the tech smart-arse who worked all the hours god sent, but would occasionally turn up near midnight with a bottle of wine and ask me to hurt her, force my whole fist inside her, or make her drink my piss. I was into basically none of that, but I quite liked having her around, so I just went along with it. Before I met Emma I sometimes worried I'd spend the rest of my life pissing on people who I wasn't entirely sure even liked me that much. A whole life spent fisting the indifferent.

From the beginning with Emma, it felt different. I remember sitting in a bar with her just after we'd first started seeing each other and realising that I just couldn't shut the fuck up. The words were clambering over one another in my throat, trying to find a way out. I could hear myself telling her about how the only thing I really liked about having money was the access it granted me to ice, about how much I bloody loved ice and how it might actually be my favourite food. And telling her about my home, about Patrick and Shiv and the girls, and how they were a genuinely good thing in the world. Just a genuinely good thing. I told her about my first job, working weekends at the petrol station. About how there was only one rule: no smoking under any circumstances. About how it was only two hours into my first shift when I was lighting my first cigarette, daydreaming about the forecourt sparking into flame and engulfing the whole estate. I remember the way the bar lights gave her shoulder blade an occasional red glow and thinking . . . *I'm fucked here, I'm totally fucked.*

By the end of that night I had decided she was the most beautiful woman I had ever seen. She made me romantic and stupid. Emma cared about the environment, so I wrote cheque after cheque to organisations that claimed to protect water or trees or air. At one fundraiser I embarrassed myself by saying that saving forests was also important so that pagans had somewhere to practise their rituals and teenagers had somewhere to wank each other off. I feel like I had a fair point—not everyone had their own bedroom growing up—but the organiser smirked at me in a way that made me feel humiliated, and then angry. When I told Emma about it in the taxi home she just laughed and then kissed me, still half laughing as her tongue found mine. And she came into my life at just the right time. My days had been getting emptier and emptier. I only ever wanted the money so I could have a different life, in a different place. And now I had it. And now Emma was in it.

Oli

The train ticket came in the post. It's a good thing that Rian messaged me and told me to look out for it, otherwise it would have just been added to the pile of unopened letters next to my door. Who the fuck is posting things these days? Putting things in little envelopes and licking a tiny bit of paper with the Queen's head on it and then walking to a post box and just throwing it in there? Anyway, apparently it still works because that's the way the train ticket turned up at my house.

It's been almost a year since we saw Rian, so we're going down to have a night out, me, Patrick and Shiv. They're getting a later train when Patrick has finished work, but I want to get there as early as I can because I fucking miss him. Patrick is great to me, Shiv too, but sometimes they treat me as if I'm one of their kids, fussing and hovering over me. Rian gets it a bit more. We're more similar than you'd think we were if you met us for the first time. We both needed to get out, so we both did. It's just that I did it without ever really leaving my sofa.

I need cans for the journey; only an idiot would pay train prices. The shops here haven't changed since I was a kid. Six of them in a semi-circle, but usually at least one of them empty or boarded up. At the far end is the church, which is only open two days a week now. On the other days the priest goes to schools and talks to assemblies of bored kids about candles or oranges or whatever it is priests talk about. At the other end is where the library used to be, but now it's a car park, or maybe just some concrete that people park their cars on. I'd totally forgotten that there used to be a library there, but Patrick kept asking people if they remembered it when we were all out for my birthday. Weird lad sometimes. Everyone high and pissed and he's shouting in our ears about the old library turning into a book van and then the book van burning down. I did remember it though. And then there's the shop everyone calls The Cave, because it is pretty dark in there and it is full of total shit. Anything you could imagine: greeting cards for weird occasions, baseball caps with fans attached to the front, plastic statues of the Virgin Mary that you can also use as a water bottle, ping pong sets, ornamental plates with cats and dogs on them, that type of stuff. We'd be in there all the time back in the day because it was so easy to steal from. You could fill your pockets while the old girl wasn't looking and come out loaded down with all sorts of things: a bag of marbles, a bouncy ball, some watch batteries, breath mints in an ornamental tin.

Six cans for the journey, but I'll open the first one on the walk to the station. Crack the second as we start moving. The carriage stays empty for the first twenty minutes or so, passing through the local stations, places where nobody really uses the train. I take the opportunity to cut out a small line on the fold-down table. Golden. The first line is always golden. Everything gets brighter by the second. Greens greener, blues bluer, reds redder. Only lines for the next twenty-four hours, no brown, I've made that promise to myself. We are supposed to be meeting Rian's new girl, and I don't want to embarrass him. Or myself, for that matter. I've been cutting down these last few months anyway, trying to level out a bit and come up for air. Conor has got some new building project on the go and offered me a few months' graft, stable and with decent money. This time I said yes. Last year I'd got to the point where I couldn't go without brown for more than about four hours, but I can manage a day or so now. If I can get it down to once every three days, I reckon the job with Conor will be O.K.

First proper station and a couple of old lads take seats near me. By my fourth can they are both asleep. I cut another small line and wonder what their lives were like when they were my age. How did you fuck up a life forty or fifty years ago? Was it in the same ways we do now, or was it all slower and steadier? Were there more chances to change your mind?

The first time I ever did a line, I was fourteen years old. I was staying with my uncle in his caravan during the summer. We called it a "holiday," but I was only really there because my mom was sick. I didn't want to be there, and he didn't want me there either. Every night that summer he'd roll back late from the pub and then he'd shake me awake so we could play game after game of cards or draughts until finally his head would start lolling to one side every few seconds and we'd both give up and go to bed. It was a bribe, I suppose: if I would crawl out of bed to play a few hands with him, he'd give me some of those ice-cold beers in stubby bottles and a few half lines to keep me awake. I can remember the feeling of the straw against my nostril, the slight burn, and then the almost overwhelming sense that I needed to stop playing cards and leave the caravan immediately. There was stuff out there! I could feel it! I would run for as long as it took to find it!

He was a rough lad, my uncle, but always good to me. Decent. He'd spent a decade in the army during his twenties, but never really spoke much about it. Except that whenever the news was on and there was talk of bombings and deployments and IEDs, he'd change the channel . . . *you don't need to see this . . . you've got enough shit on your plate without hearing about that bollocks.* That's just what he was like.

We were out driving once and there was a dead fox by the side of the road. He told me it was sleeping, that foxes always slept by the side of the road. He said that even though I could clearly see the fox's guts hanging out, red lakes on black tarmac. First line and first fuck in that caravan. A girl I don't remember, falling on her, hurried, frantic, her elbow accidentally bloodying my gum. Asking afterwards if it counted and her saying it did. Not telling Patrick or Conor or Rian about it when I got home because I knew full well they wouldn't believe me.

Fifth beer down and we're there. Into the city. Crazy here, but I like it. Everyone's factory settings are two notches higher, hurrying, needing to be somewhere. I'm in everyone's way because I keep stopping to look at things. I don't mind one bit. They can take the extra two seconds and go around me. It's O.K. to look at things. No horizon here, or at least not one you can see. The buildings are too tall, which is fucking weird if you think about it, not right to live without ever being able to see the horizon. I can't quite get this street dance right, I'm too slow and too pissed, lacking the rhythm and the timing that comes when you properly know a place. But I make it in the end. Rian's flat. All glass, like one of those old-fashioned cola bottles that people pay double for even though they are smaller than the plastic ones. The man at the desk has my name on a list, which is probably the only list I've ever been on that isn't because I'm in trouble for something. I throw my arms around Rian, slapping his back over and over. He looks good. Getting a bit fat, the last few buttons of his shirt straining over his stomach. It suits him. He looks good. He looks happy.

Patrick

For the first time in my life, I feel nervous about seeing Rian. Or maybe it's not *seeing* him so much as it is seeing him *there*, in his new world. I'm used to him coming to us, coming home. Shiv is excited. Excited to leave the girls for a night, excited to be doing something different. There's an edge to her, though. Some nerves of her own, maybe. Makes me promise we won't leave her talking to Rian's new girlfriend all night. But once the train is moving, edging its way through the handful of local stops before it properly picks up speed, I can feel us both start to relax. I'm looking at Shiv, sitting across from me with her head pressed against the train window, letting the vibrations work their way through her skull. I want to make a joke about it being a poor man's massage or something, but I can't quite make the joke work, maybe because these train tickets are really fucking expensive. Still, there was no way I'd let Rian pay. It is good to see Shiv like this, in a different context.

Nothing to do for the next two hours but look at her. Relook at her. Remember her. All the versions of her I've loved over the years, packed together in front of me, forehead shaking against a Perspex window.

It's dark by the time we get off the train and throw ourselves into the current of the city. I remember instantly how much I hate this place. It fools you at first; it seems full of bright glass and light, sun in the morning and neon at night. But if you're willing to stare, or squint, or even to just stand still and look for a few minutes, it starts to feel like something else entirely. It starts to feel thick and cloying, like a dense forest of black trees, webbed together with thick, sticky oil. Seriously, if you showed a kid a picture of this city skyline and asked them where the evil people lived, they'd point straight to the beating heart of it, to its tallest buildings, to exactly where it keeps its gold. None of that tonight though, none of my misery talk. We are here to see Rian. I stand at the side of the road with my arm in the air, waiting for a car to take us right to him. Straight to his door.

Rian looks good. Fat and happy. He has the shape of someone who is enjoying things, the shape of someone who only stops when they are properly full. It's nice to see. He's the only soft thing in this place though; the rest of his flat is all hard lines and absence. It looks like a fucking show home. White marble surfaces with nothing on them, a white sofa with no cushions, polished wood floors with no rug and floor-to-ceiling windows that make it feel like you're outside, hovering above the city and waiting to fall. If you exclude Oli, who is practically bouncing off the walls by the time me and Shiv get there, the place feels totally lifeless. It's weird that he chose this, when he could have chosen anything. Because when we were kids, Rian's house was always the one that was bursting at the seams, full of people and voices and laughter and arguments. At least until the later years. His old man started to get quiet and angry towards the end. That house got sadder then. I still feel a bit guilty about how we all started to drift away when that happened. There's a certain level of drunk where I always want to say something about that, apologise, but I know he'd hate it, so I've always managed to swallow the sorrys down.

The four of us are drinking beer on Rian's balcony, everyone on chairs apart from Oli, who is hanging half over the railing and has decided to shout his contributions into the traffic. Christ I love him, the mad fucker. It might be my imagination but I think he might even be looking a bit healthier as well. Shiv is smoking one of Oli's cigarettes, arching her neck back and taking deep, long, hungry drags. I haven't seen her smoke in years. She gave up when she first got pregnant and I remember taking months to adjust to the new way her skin and tongue tasted. It's nice to watch her like this. As if someone has idly flicked the hands of the clock back and we are ten years younger for the night, less certain about the way our life is going to be.

I tell Rian that the project he gave Conor money for is the talk of the Trident, all the old boys wondering if the new flats might block their view . . . *their view? Fucking hell, their view of what exactly?!* But Oli chips in, turning away from the traffic for a second . . . *they mean the sky, obviously . . . they're used to seeing the sky.* Fair enough. I can tell that Rian doesn't care about the flats, that it's just one more iron in the fire for him. But he perks up a bit when he finds out Oli will be working on the site, and when I tell him that Conor has seemed two feet taller this last year. With his new project and his new son. I say this even though I have no idea if it's true. I need to see more of Conor, not let him drift.

An hour or so more up there and then we head to the bar. Rian's new girlfriend (*Emma, Emma, trying to make her name stick . . .*) will meet us there. On the way we must pass ten delivery riders, anonymous and familiar in standard-issue jacket and mask. On a different night each of them could be me. Might as well be me. Is me. Be your own boss, they say. But I'm not my own boss, am I? Because if I actually *were* my own boss I'd pay myself more and give myself more time off, wouldn't I? Your own boss. I mean, come on, fucking hell. I'll be glad when the robots come, genuinely. When there's an army of drones precision-bombing burgers into new build flats and scattering fries over the city like salty rain. They can do that and I can get on with doing something else with my life. Anything else, for that matter. I'm glad that neither Oli nor Rian make any comment about the riders as they pass. It would throw me off, and I want to be happy tonight, I want it to be easy, I want to find the fulcrum of things, stop everything tilting and spinning, just for a few hours.

SHIV

It's the type of place where people bring drinks to your table. Before tonight, I've never been somewhere where you don't have to queue at the bar. When I was younger, I would have hated this. Going to the bar was the time you got to see who else was around, feel people's eyes on you, maybe get talking to someone you didn't know. I used to like the scrum, the jostle, the closeness. Going to the bar was sort of the whole point, for me. But not tonight. Tonight I'm glad of it, glad of the eager, fussy waiter. Glad to be with Oli and Patrick and Rian, and not to have to waste time away from them.

By the time Emma finally joins us, we are all a few drinks deep. She is striking, and I can feel Patrick trying his best not to stare at her as she moves around the table and greets everyone by kissing them on the cheek. Seven kisses total, one on each cheek for the visitors and one on the mouth for Rian. She is noticeably tall, and her satin dress clings to the outline of her long leg muscles. You know the way advertisers sometimes make cartoon foxes or rabbits look a bit human and also massively sexy? Emma is exactly like that, except this time they have done it with a praying mantis. That's it. Emma looks like a really sexy cartoon praying mantis. And her eyes. They are that papery green with brown flecks you only see on the skin of overripe pears. She keeps leaning over to say things to me. Banal things mostly, flat and distant but friendly. Fucking hell. She smells like pears as well. Ridiculous.

I was worried I'd be a bit anxious around her, but I'm not.

She's nice enough, but she's also a bit silly and the least fun person at our table. At least, she is to me. Patrick and Oli are laughing way too much at everything she says, that type of eager politeness that is just about transparent enough that you can see the lust showing underneath. I'm drunk enough that I want to dance, but it doesn't really seem that type of place; I can't see anyone else dancing. Imagine that, you spend money on a night out and you don't even get to spin around like an idiot for a bit. Maybe it will liven up later, or maybe there's another room upstairs. If not, maybe Emma will loosen up a bit and we can all dance when we get back to the flat. It's been so long since I've been out without having to worry about sorting Molly and Freya the next morning, I'll be fucked if I'm going to waste it.

Rian is telling Emma a story about something that happened when we were all about fifteen. He's leaning in too much, speaking a bit too loud, looking at her a bit too intently, gauging her response. The poor bastard is gulping her down like he is parched, and I can just tell that something in her is recoiling a bit . . . *so, Conor swings at this guy, hands around his neck, and before we know it, the whole chip shop is fighting, punches flying everywhere* . . . Emma smiles, just about. *And then out of nowhere, Oli starts shouting, Rian! Rian! look at this! . . . and when I turn around he's waving this prosthetic leg above his head! He's kicked this bloke in the leg and the bloke's fake leg has come clean off! He's waving it above his head like a staff or something, as if he's Moses and he is going to lead us into the promised land and start parting the waves with this prosthetic leg! . . .* Emma smiles. Again, just about. Oli starts protesting . . . *I wouldn't do that now, by the way . . . I was only a kid. Feel a bit bad about it, thinking back . . . you can't take the piss out of cripples by waving their fake legs about. Actually, I feel really bad about that. Really bad. You've got to stop telling the leg story, mate . . . I'm deadly serious.* Oli's earnestness breaks through any residual tension, thank god, and everyone is folded over laughing, apart from

Emma. The more we open up, the more it seems to shut her down. I'm gutted for Rian. For love-struck Rian, in his shirt that looks at least a size too small. The music seems to get louder. I can feel it thrashing through me.

It's hard not to feel protective. Rian keeps putting his head on Emma's shoulders, trying to draw her out a bit. His heavy skull on her pale skin, a dumb wasp headbutting a newly cleaned window. I want to tell her to grow the fuck up, to lighten the fuck up, to give him something back. I want to tell her that it isn't enough to just be beautiful, that even the best of us are only granted a few summers of it before it is taken from us. All faces have a destiny, and none of them are good.

We obviously pass some sort of enjoyment threshold, because at some point Emma decides we should all leave and head back to the flat. There is an hour until last orders and every part of me wants to stay where the music is, where the noise is. I'm pissed enough to risk it. *Ah, come on Emma, live a little . . . let's stay until they throw us out . . . we're not dead yet.* To my surprise, Rian falls in behind . . . *Shiv is right, we don't get to do this often enough, let's stay for one more.* But we don't stay for one more. There are words uttered behind hands and then there is an announcement that we are, in fact, leaving after all. There is coldness on the walk back, Oli and Patrick too far gone to notice it. I try a few times to ease it, inane observations, questions to Emma which I couldn't really care less about. It doesn't work.

So there are a few more beers back on Rian's balcony. And a couple of lines once Oli is drunk enough not to care what Emma might think. It's a good night, just about. But by about 3 A.M., I'm the only one left up, pressed against the balcony and watching the ash from my cigarette fall on the city. Weird place really. This late at night and you can still hear the cars and the trains. And every few minutes someone walks past the building opposite and triggers a sensor that bathes them in white light, as if they have been chosen for the rapture. Eventually, I give in and head inside. Shoes off and tiptoeing across Rian's hardwood floor and past his ridiculous fridge that I know full well he only uses as an ice dispenser. Patrick is asleep, cleaved to one side of the oversized bed. I consider waking him; it would be nice to have sex without worrying about one of the girls barging in, but I can't bring myself to deprive him of sleep. He's a good man. He looks small, curled up like that. Partly because the bed is so big, but also because he's lost weight recently, his back less broad, veins starting to show a bit in his forearms and hands. I've slept next to him almost every night for fifteen years. Since we were kids, basically. There has never been anyone else. Not really.

Like most couples, we had our moments, especially when we were younger. Hard times, times when I wasn't sure if we'd make it, times when I wasn't sure this was enough. Times I thought I might want a different type of life, whatever that meant. And I've done stupid things. I'm sure Patrick has too. I don't mind that, not deep down, not really. A few kisses and a few crushes over the years, which we'd both always end up confessing and forgiving. The only thing I'd never tell Patrick, the only thing I've properly buried, is what happened the year he went away to university. We'd broken up for a while, a few months maybe. Neither of us could afford the train fare back and forth and it felt like we might end up just drifting apart. Sometimes I can even feel it still lingering in the flat, what happened, giving off a sweet rot that only I can smell. But only sometimes. At the end of his first year his mom got sick and he came home to look after her. By the time she died I was pregnant with Molly, and that was that. I was showing at the funeral, hoping nobody noticed my dress was too tight, wondering what it meant for us.

Patrick rolls over in his sleep, drapes his arm across my chest. I realise I won't be able to sleep now. One too many lines. Maybe better to just push through. Tomorrow might be easier to face on adrenaline alone. I'm already starting to regret letting the night get away from me and I can feel anxiety about tomorrow starting to close in. Swallow it down. Might as well wait for the sun. Wait for the sound of ice rattling out of Rian's ridiculous fridge. Wait for the sound of Oli's voice going a hundred miles an hour. Wait for the coffee to brew. For the train home.

Rian

I first decided to leave the estate on the day we put Patrick's mom in the ground. The feel of wet soil on my fingers and then the sound of it hitting the wood . . . *and now we will undertake the funeral sacrament* . . . Patrick looking straight ahead, his chin tilted slightly higher than usual, performing his part, play-acting his strength . . . *the right of commendation is designed to* . . . The same old faces, the same hands patting his shoulder as they headed past him and into the church . . . *absolution is the process by which* . . . Shiv by his side, starting to show under her black dress, slight enough that it probably only registered with those who already knew. And the worst of it. That even then, at that moment, as my best friend buried his mother, I could feel myself burning a bit for what they had. I was disgusted with myself. A family changing hands in front of me, the old passing away and making way for the new, and I was there burning up, clinging to scraps and shards, pathetic. It was time to leave. Time to leave the funeral and time to leave that place. I remember thinking that there just weren't enough good things there, that there just wasn't enough joy. And that because there wasn't enough, everyone ended up making themselves sick fighting over the scraps.

We had done the same with my old man, years before. Lowered him into the ground, thrown the soil, patted the shoulders. Where we grew up, people usually seemed to either die young doing something stupid or die too soon because their body gave in, but if they made it past the danger zone, they seemed to hang on for ever, creeping around the shops for eternity on electric wheelchairs or walking frames. My old man was in the middle category. His body gave in first and then the pain made his mind give in as well. We never really found out what was wrong with him, but Patrick used to call it shit-life syndrome. Just fucking sediments of shit that eventually become too much. Never enough money, never enough time, too many days spent carrying things and breaking things, too many fumes in the street, too many fumes at work, too little sleep, too much worry, stress pumping through your veins for fifty years like a black river. It made sense to me.

He didn't leave much when he died, but once I'd cleared the stuff he owed and sold the house there was about forty grand left. I spent five on mindless shit straight away, spent it because I was missing him and because I was angry at myself for never speaking to him properly, for never loving him properly. But after that, I clung to the money that was left as if my life depended on it. I knew it meant I could leave when the time came. And the time had come that day, when I found myself staring at Patrick and Shiv like a cunt, not being able to get past my own needs, my own greed. I didn't know what I'd do when I left, but I assumed I'd figure it out. I'd always been good at buying things and selling things, ever since I was a kid. I'd just do that. Use the money I had, buy some things, sell them for more than I paid, and then do it again. I'd do that until I had a new life, until I had some joy of my own and could start loving people properly without feeling like I needed to steal theirs.

Those first days in the city, edging around it slowly as if I were carrying something heavy. Finally understanding what people meant when they said they had a knot in their stomach, something coiled and ready to unravel. I remember buying a notebook, for the first time in my life, because I had an idea that was what you did when you needed to figure things out: you got a notebook and wrote in it until things got clearer. Sitting in cafes and bars for weeks on end with my empty notebook until carrying it about started to piss me off so much that I tore the pages out one by one and practised throwing them into the bin I had in my room.

Like an idiot, I'd thought my room was some sort of bargain that everybody else had missed, cheaper than everything else I looked at but also much closer to the centre of the city. But by the time the first weekend had rolled around, I'd already figured out why. Turns out when people said it was good to *live central*, they didn't mean the *actual* centre, which come 7 P.M. was an utter wasteland. Abandoned bars shedding customers eager to get the trains back to the suburbs, and not even bothering to open at all from Friday to Sunday. In those first few weeks, it was the same conversation every time . . . *oh, you actually mean the "City?" I didn't realise people actually lived around there, I thought it was all banks.* I quickly learned to not mention it. Initially, I didn't touch the money I'd brought with me. I clung to it. I was making just about enough to live by playing online poker against Americans who seemed to be happy to lose again and again as long as you didn't beat them too quickly. It was easiest if you played when it was about eleven or midnight on the east coast, to catch them while they were drunk and tired. Before long, I was making almost a grand a week that way, long nights but easy money. I remember thinking, this will do. I could just ebb out the rest of my life here until I got bored enough to jump in the fucking river. I'd already left the estate, and that seemed like enough, like an end point in itself. The leaving was the whole point. I wasn't going to die where I was born.

After about six months I got bored of counting cards, of watching the same four shapes turning on a loop. I moved on to stocks, it was simpler, just buying and selling, no need to imagine a human being on the other side, face lit up by a laptop screen, waiting for you to act, for you to choose. I wasn't that good at first; I'd make a bit, then lose a bit, generally coming out more or less even. I didn't mind that. Not losing was enough. But by the time the first winter arrived, with its days that seemed to last no more than an hour at most, I felt that familiar urge, my hand hovering over the big red button that said *fuck it*. I started buying warrants. Warrants are stupid things. If a normal share is a pint, a warrant is more like a massive line of speed: high risk, volatile, erratic. They could often end up totally worthless within a day. Like a dickhead, I spent half of everything I had on twenty thousand of them. Every time they rose by a penny, I made five grand, and every time they fell by a penny, I lost the same amount. A coin flip, basically. I watched them go up and down for two weeks, dreaming blank dreams and feeling like I had eaten nothing except plate after plate of noisy birds.

By the fourteenth day they were all gone; half the money my old man had spent his whole life building was gone in fourteen days. When I saw the ticker finally hit zero I felt sick. And then I actually was sick. Retching out weeks of stress and bile until I was properly empty. But by the time the pitiful winter sun had crept up the buildings opposite, I'd lumped the rest on, gamblers' fallacy. *Fuck it. Fuck it.* Everything I had on twenty thousand more warrants. The coin started to land differently this time, tilting on its edge and then falling my way, over and over. By the time I cashed those warrants out, three months later, I'd made four hundred thousand. More money than my old man would have seen in his entire life.

And that was enough to change everything. That money has been making me money ever since. More. Much more. And now, five years down the line, my days are full of people just offering me new ways to make the numbers go even higher . . . *a million from you today, with a guaranteed 3X in eighteen months* . . . It's fucking stupid, and after a while it makes you feel embarrassed as well. The ease of it. Or maybe I was always embarrassed about it, deep down. After that first time, that first four hundred thousand, it took me ages to go home, to see everyone again. I felt like I had something to admit, to confess. I felt like I'd stolen it, or like I'd stolen something at least. When I eventually said all this to Patrick he just laughed and said I probably felt like I'd stolen the money because I basically *had* stolen it. Maybe he's right. But most days I'm O.K. with it. It's just buying and selling. And eating all the ice I could possibly want. And looking at the river. It's just buying things and selling things and eating ice while you look at the river. That's what it all amounts to. And that is fine.

Conor

When Sean finally arrived it wasn't anything like I thought it would be. In the first days after he was born he wouldn't eat, and the house filled up with his screams until the midwife finally took him and Sophie back into hospital for a few nights. I tried to do the practical things. Clean things, buy things, ferry things back and forth to their ward. But nothing felt like enough and by the time they were well enough to come home, it was hard not to feel like I'd failed them already. Like I'd been given a perfect gift and then fumbled it straight away. And something else had happened too. I thought having a child would help stitch me back together a bit, make me less frayed at the edges, but instead it began pulling at my seams, unpicking me, opening up wounds quicker than I could cauterise them shut. So I focused on the building. Kept busy. Building I knew how to do. I knew how to make a building grow; I knew how to make a building safe.

I'm excited for Rian to see the project. He was supposed to come and check in last month, just after they'd all gone to visit him, but ended up cancelling at the last minute. It was no bad thing, to be honest; four more weeks of progress have put us in a better place. That's one of the things about buildings: it can look like nothing is happening for months on end and then almost overnight the fucker just springs up out of nowhere. Or maybe that's how everything happens. Maybe that is the literal definition of happening, lots of nothing and then suddenly something. Either way, it seems especially true of buildings, because it's the foundations that take forever, the stuff you can see is the easy bit.

I'm glad not to be showing Rian around a building site that is only foundations and groundworks and anchoring. I'm glad the outline of the flats is starting to show. I'll tell him things are going well, which they mostly are. A few supply issues, a few people have let me down, but generally things are just about O.K. I'll need to ask him for a bit more money, liquidity really, just to tide things over until we sell the first few units off plan. I know he won't mind; he'll be pleased to see things shaping up. And anyway, he gets these things, he gets that projects like this can exist on a knife edge: a few missteps and then you're deep in the red. He won't let that happen. But overall, I'm proud of it, a busy site feels good and for once I'm not being treated like shit and bossed around by some old prick who doesn't know what he's doing. This is my thing. New era. Starting to make things happen, taking care of my family, money for Sean, money for Sophie if she needs it. Finish this project and then on to the next. I've even started to like it when the old lads in the pub moan at me. Asking the same questions every time, telling me it's ruining their view or that it's blocking the fucking sun or making the sky look ugly. When people who hate change moan about things changing, it might mean things are actually changing. And thank god for that.

Rian turns up in a car that I am dying to take the piss out of. Baby blue and built for somebody half his size. He unfolds himself limb by limb and looks miserable enough that I decide to save the piss-taking for later. His girlfriend gets out of the other door. It's hard to know if she's as miserable as him because she's got a scarf wrapped around most of her face. It's a cold day but the stealth-assassin look still seems a bit much to me. You can practically see them shaking off whatever is bothering them as they walk towards the site, and by the time they're close enough to speak we are all smiles and kisses on the cheek and pleased-to-meet-yous. Emma says she has heard all about me and like a total prick I can feel myself saying that thing people always say in response . . . *only good things I hope?!* Fuck me. I show them around but after about ten minutes or so Emma says she'll wait in the car and then join us in a bit for coffee. Bit standoffish, but she smelled incredible. The whole site smells like toast and potato waffles, of all the orange foods except actual oranges. But she smelled like actual fruit. Wet, clean, cold, fruit.

I ask Rian if he can picture what used to be here, if he can remember how creepy the Meadows was, and that time we tried to break in but lost our nerve. He doesn't seem that interested and I can feel he isn't listening to me properly. It's like a knife in the neck that he doesn't give a fuck. Means the world to me and it's all a formality to him. Now's not the time to ask for more money, obviously. The only time he smiles is when he hears Oli shouting down at him from the scaffold on the other side of the site . . . *no rich twats allowed on the site unless they're buying me a coffee . . . and is that your car, that little blue thing? I'm sorry mate, I'm going to have to burn it immediately, it's for your own good . . .* I'm always glad to have Oli around. But I'm especially glad right at that second.

Coffee it is. Oli playing the jester, playing the poet . . . *you know how I take mine. Dark as the night sky on a dark and starless night, endless dark, a big black hole in a big white mug.* Social glue, that lad. Barely keeping it together, brain half collapsed from all the brown and he can still read a room better than any of us. We eat our lunch in this cafe every day; it hasn't changed in twenty years, and it probably hasn't been cleaned for about ten either. We used to come in here for fry-ups the morning after a big night, or every now and then at the tail end of a massive one that had run straight through to morning. We'd sit there with the shivers and sweats, laughing until we couldn't breathe, until somebody laughed so much they coughed up some half-chewed bread onto the table and ruined our appetites. The same prayer mat hanging up behind the counter, a spiderweb of coloured threads that looked perfect when you still had enough of the night before in your system, literally perfect. And the same faded print on the wall, its white frame turned yellow from years of grease. The picture is of one of the old blocks of flats, half collapsed by a controlled demolition, sinking back into its footprint and into the earth. The clouds of dust and concrete seemed to be hanging in mid-air, resisting gravity, and if you stared hard enough they started to take on the shape of mountains, covered in clouds and mist. I loved that picture. We used to all go and watch the demolitions when we were kids; they were the most exciting things we'd ever seen, it felt like watching a magic trick on a massive scale. Oli once told me you could see Satan in the clouds of dust if you looked hard enough, an angel kicked out of heaven, tumbling to the earth like lightning. But to me it was always simpler than that. Just something disappearing. The end of a future that never quite happened.

We stay for exactly as long as it takes to make, serve, drink and pay for a round of coffees and then Rian and Emma are gone. I didn't get to say any of the things I needed to say.

A few hours later, Sophie and I are sitting with Patrick and Shiv and I'm trying to avoid telling them all of the things I never got to say to Rian. How I might need a bit more money to see it through properly, and how it takes so long because the foundations are the hard work. Patrick always gets weird about houses though, thinks they should *sit outside of the market* or some such bollocks, and luckily that is enough to get me to keep my mouth shut. Sophie already thinks I'm useless, doesn't let me anywhere near Sean some days. Most of the time I think she's being unreasonable, but occasionally I wonder if she might be right, that maybe she can see a poison in me and doesn't want me spilling it everywhere when I speak. Patrick and Shiv look so easy with each other, so beautiful. It makes me want to rip open their life with my bare hands and see how it all works. I've got all the parts for a life, but it doesn't seem to be working quite right. I need to see inside, see the mechanisms, that way I could fix things. They are talking and laughing about their trip to the city to see Rian. I nod along but I can't quite keep up . . . *I think there was something off about Emma . . . Patrick disagrees but that's only because he couldn't stop staring at her . . . honestly the place was so empty . . . like a morgue . . . no, actually, not a morgue, it was more like the way you might imagine a posh mental hospital in the 1950s . . .* Sean breaks up the conversation with his crying, so I take the opportunity to hold him while I can. My son, his warm, wet breath against my face, the most beautiful thing I know, but I'm not entirely sure who is comforting who.

Rian

Hard to know where an end begins. But something was off that day we went back to see Conor and check in on the building project. If I run the film backwards and pay really close attention, then maybe I can trace it back a bit further. A drip in the ceiling that is quiet enough that you don't notice it until there is water pooling at your feet. Emma was always reluctant to leave the city, there was always something there that couldn't be missed, someone who was in town but only for the night, some gravitational pull that kept us there for months at a time. This time it was more than that, more than inertia. There was something about stepping back into my past that seemed to repulse her, make her want to look away. I think Emma would have preferred it if I came from nowhere, had no background, no origin, was just a cipher that turned up in her life fully formed, grown in a fucking petri dish. The whole time we were there I could feel her recoiling, as if the place might leave some grease on her that she wouldn't be able to wash off, that people would be able to smell on her when she got back.

I hated it, because I'd wanted her to see my home, wanted her to love the things that I loved. I'd wanted to empty everything out, crack myself open and shovel all the mud out onto the table . . . *Look at all that shit, when you look at it do you still love me?* . . . I wanted to start talking and never stop, babble on about babies and buildings and beasts and virgins. But we just stood there, surrounded by concrete and steel and bricks, and I could feel something starting to turn. We left early. I'd wanted to tell her about the picture in the cafe, how weird it was that we used to all go and watch the houses and flats get demolished for fun, like a cinema that only showed one really short, really violent film. The whole day was heavy . . . *I just don't get why you always want to come back to this, it's done now* . . . Everything felt like an accusation, like she'd sensed some sort of fatal flaw . . . *You don't even have any family there any more, it's not healthy to live in the past* . . . I just kept driving, folded up inside the ridiculously small car, and folding up even smaller every time she said something. It didn't stop and I couldn't reply, more concrete pouring out, filling the back seat and sliding down my throat . . . *Can we turn the music off? I'm trying to talk to you.* I've never known how people can drive without music playing; without it you can feel the road beneath you, feel the speed shambling through your bones. I'm nine years old and I'm in confession, wanting to speak, I'm eleven years old and I'm in confession, wanting to spill out every one of my sins . . . *can we just keep the music on for now? . . . it helps me to concentrate . . . just for a bit.*

And that night they all came to visit, the way Emma acted as though she had been invaded somehow. As if they were interlopers crossing the border and bringing dirt and disease with them. She'd hated that I sided with Shiv about staying out a bit longer; it was such a nothing exchange, but it lingered between us for days. A betrayal of something, as though I'd revealed some sick fealty to my old life. Words that are hard to take back . . . *the trouble with you, Rian, is that you love your scars, you have favourite wounds that you just like to uncover and look at as though they were art.* There was more like that. Variations on a theme. That I was loyal to the wrong things, the wrong people, that I'd never really left.

You know how when you love somebody you can always sort of feel where they are? I've always thought of it as string, but I don't suppose everybody does. The important thing is that you can always feel it, connecting you. They can be somewhere else, doesn't matter where, doing something else, doesn't matter what, but all the time you can feel it, endless and weightless, binding your movements together. Well, in the weeks after Emma and I got back from visiting Conor I could feel that string getting slacker and slacker, fraying and breaking. I imagined a faceless man, on the other side of the city, absent-mindedly rolling one of those ridiculous little suitcases over it and snapping the last of its threads. It was as if, all at once, after weeks of expecting her to call, to come round late at night, I knew with total certainty that she wouldn't, and that I'd never see her again.

It doesn't help when you have nothing to do. And I had nothing to do. Not a fucking thing. That was the whole point to begin with, to get to a place where there was nothing I had to do. To wake up in the morning and be confronted by a sort of blank desire, completely unmoored from need and necessity. There are some people I've met these last few years who claim that they love the game, that they love making money just for the sake of it, but I don't really think they mean it. What they really mean is that they want to get so good at the game that they can choose whether or not they ever have to play it again and whether or not their kids and grandkids ever have to play it again. They love the game so much they want to be able to leave it for dead whenever they feel like it. I never loved the game, I just wanted to get to the other side, to see what I wanted when I didn't have anything left to need. I was so sick of fucking needing things, that's why I started all this. But now what? I spend days on my balcony, imagining that the river or the light or the glass might give me answers. I *want* to want to be near the ocean or to feel a particular sort of grass under my feet or a particular sort of wind on my face, but I don't want any of those things. Sometimes you just have to let the end of things breathe. Just shut the fuck up and eat it.

So I let the end of things breathe. And I shut the fuck up. And I eat it. There isn't drama, there are just no words where there used to be words and no skin where there used to be skin and that's it. I start to hate the image of myself in this barren flat, getting fatter and fatter even though I feel like I'm only ever eating ice. There's nothing left here for me, no anchors; I could leave tomorrow and it wouldn't matter. Phone my secretary and tell her I'm selling up, cashing out, no more meetings. And anyway, aren't you supposed to go home at the end of the story, after you've conquered whatever it is you left home to conquer? Aren't I supposed to ride into town with an animal corpse on my back? I start to think I should go home, see if there are things there to hang on to. I start to think I can undo things, that I can figure out if there is anything left to want. I start to think I should let all the bruises bloom or they'll turn my blood bad. And I start to wait up every night for that moment when the sky first starts to slightly brighten and bleed. Oh, and I start to fall to pieces.

Three

Patrick

I don't know how long I've been asleep. I feel Shiv shaking my shoulder, reaching into my dreams and pulling me up into the air of the bedroom. She hands me the phone, her breath warm and sour against my face . . . *it's Rian, I think he's pissed.* He starts out light, he's all . . . *unexpected trip and spur of the moment and live a little and I miss you.* But I can sense something thick and awkward catching in his voice. Three or four interruptions later, three or four . . . *seriously, are you O.Ks* . . . and finally he asks me outright. Doesn't want to be alone, needs company, needs to see a familiar face. And my answer is yes. My answer is always yes.

It sounds so quiet where he is, the way I imagine it might if he'd called from a home recording studio, with the walls covered in egg cartons, or from a padded cell in an abandoned infirmary. It's probably the expensive furniture in his hotel room. Expensive furniture eats sound, just sucks it all in. That's what the word plush means really, plush means whispering. Distracting myself as I pull on my trousers in the darkness. Or there's the other type of expensive furniture, the type that is thin and brittle. That type does the opposite, makes everything shrill and loud. That's what the word minimal means, really, minimal means screaming. I switch on the light in the kitchen, drink a glass of water and look at the clock. Coming up to 2 A.M. I'm fucked, lead heavy. Stirring heaped spoons of instant coffee into boiling water and drinking it as quickly as the heat will let me. *Just jumping on the bike now, I'll be with you in about forty* minutes. The door clicks behind me. Music filling up my ears as I build up speed on the empty roads. Fast enough that the shop signs are a blur of blue and green as I pass. Just colour, I pretend I don't already know what the signs say. *Room 437, door is already open.*

I find Rian on the bathroom floor, head in his hands. He doesn't look up at me until I ask him to. He looks like shit: purple rings under both his eyes, pale skin. A face like two old plums pressed against newspaper. He looks like someone who has had way too much and not nearly enough, all at once. I kneel down next to him and he starts to talk, slow at first, as if his tongue is too thick for his mouth . . . *I couldn't make it work . . . I did all of the right things. I did things. You know when you're eating something that doesn't taste of anything and eventually you just get bored of it . . . even though you are fucking starving . . . you just can't keep putting your spoon in it and lifting it to your mouth over and over again . . . she knew there was something wrong with me and I think she's right. I did all the right things but she could fucking smell it on me. After enough time has passed, you just start biting down on the metal of the spoon . . . just to taste something different. Mate . . . I feel fucking ashamed. The string just broke. I can't believe I dragged you all the way out here on your fucking bike . . . I think she was right you know. Mate, I'm so sorry.*

A few false starts, reaching for the right thing to say. There will be some combination of sounds I can make with my face that will make things better. I just have to find them. I tell him that I liked Emma and that I understand why he's in pain and that she will probably come around. This doesn't work. So I tell him that Shiv sensed something off with her from the beginning and that he is probably better off without her. This doesn't work either. I tell him that none of us actually knew Emma and that sometimes we all cling to things that we shouldn't . . . *you don't want to end up like one of those weird lads that spends their time trying to catch butterflies in nets and then pinning them in little glass cases . . .* I'm rambling at him, pivoting, ricocheting, trying to find the right way forward. Rian stands up and braces himself against the sink, and I start to realise this probably isn't just about Emma. It feels like something important is coming loose, working its way free.

Animal sounds, as if he is trying to hold in a scream or swallow a howl. *I did everything right. There's something bad in me I think . . . the string just broke. Fuck me, this is embarrassing . . . just let me get it out . . .* So I do. I watch this man I have known all my life hold on to a sink, grip it until his hands go white and cry pints of tears. And when it finally ebbs and then finally stops, I put my arms around him . . . *how fucking soft is this shirt? Are rich people wearing young people's skin now? . . . because if you are I think that might be a bit on the fucking nose . . .* Under the fat, the muscles of his back, movement, maybe laughter, or something like it. How long has he been here like this? Hours or days? There's a faint stink to him. Poor bastard. Breathing properly now. Embarrassed smile. I reckon he could do with leaving this room . . . *let's get a bit of air. The sun will be up soon enough, we could even watch it . . . bit of romance.* Probably not . . . *Fuck off Patrick . . . I'd genuinely rather watch a paedophile do a jigsaw.* Fair enough. So drinking it is.

Something we are good at. The grooves are already worn into the soil. Glass after glass, hotel wine in a silver bucket . . . *you should keep hold of the bucket, Rian, you could cry into it later if the mood takes you . . .* I fill him in. Tell him about Conor and Sophie, how their kid is sweet but I think there's something going on there that Conor won't talk about . . . *he's always at the building site, doesn't matter what time I ride past there, I think he's avoiding going home. Anyway, he'll be glad you're back for a bit.* Rian listens, but only just, and doesn't say much in return. I notice he is scratching at his ankle constantly; it looks red raw as if he is about to break the skin and draw blood.

Fucking stop that. Slap his hand. *It's like drinking with a homeless dog . . . hang on, aren't all dogs homeless, in a way?*

When he finally starts speaking, the words just keep coming. Unravelling. Years of him, peeling away, flaking off like old paint. Renouncing things, Catholic drunk, sorry for this and sorry for that and sorry for the state of the world. Let him talk. Empty himself out. But then he starts saying things he shouldn't be saying, dragging up old stories, picking at old scabs. And then finally he says something that makes me want to grab the empty wine bottle, smash it against the table and push it into his face. Just to stop him talking.

Rian

Not much to take. One of the benefits of having a flat with nothing in it. Maybe I always knew I would leave in a hurry. Maybe that's why I kept the paper clean, left the crayons in the box. Everything I give a fuck about, I can fit in this stupid, tiny car. My laptop, some tailored shirts that I've got too fat for, a couple of nice suits that hide the fact I've got too fat for the shirts and some trainers that Patrick said I was at least ten years too old for the last time he visited . . . *and another thing, you know that slogan . . . just do it? . . . it comes from the final words of a serial killer, right before he was hanged . . . remember that next time you think about buying a pair of stupid trainers*. Everything in the car. Everything in the fucking tiny car that I need to get rid of as soon as possible.

I had visions of how it would be, driving out of the city, visions of what leaving would be like. I imagined the buildings melting around me and disappearing and the feeling of heading towards the edge of something. I imagined the feeling of crossing a boundary, a moment of knowing that something important was behind me. Fuck it, some dramatic sky as well, why not? A sky the colour of war. Red and orange and vital and alive. But it is none of those things. Straight away it is hot, unmoving traffic, stopping and starting but mostly stopping, brutal noise and my skin getting so sticky it reminds me of the type of lip gloss the girls used to wear when I was at school. Except in this instance it has been applied to the hairy back of a slightly overweight man in a tiny car, sitting in traffic and trying to keep his hands steady. The traffic gives me too much time, too long to talk myself around . . . *why go back, what are you picking at, what do you expect to happen?* But the voice never gets quite loud enough to make me turn back. Eventually things start to clear. More starts than stops. There is road in front of me; I have enough money to do what I want for as long as I want. I turn the radio to a station that plays music with no words. I know what I get like; my brain is as sticky as my back, and it will latch on to words like they're messages. Loud music, but no words.

I'll stay in a hotel for now, for a few weeks at least. For the first time in years I ask for a room on one of the lower floors. I want some time not thinking about the city the way I've trained myself to think of cities. I don't want to see its shape; I don't want to see which parts of it are growing and which are shrinking or whether there might be money to be made meeting new needs for basic things. I just want to be in it for a bit, just in the city. I want the people and the smells and the weird words and the being told to fuck off every two minutes. Just some breathing. In and out. The furniture in the hotel room is heavy and white, clean bones wrapped in thick towels. I lie there and let the feeling of the journey fall away, let things begin to move and rearrange in me. What the fuck is here? The people I know, Conor and Oli and Patrick and Shiv, good things. Good things that I need to learn to love properly. There's the ghost of my old man and the faces of the old lads in the Trident that always seem to summon him up. The people I used to know but don't any more. What the fuck am I scratching at. What the fuck happened to the last ten years?

Two bottles and three lines later and I am heaving tears. Bawling, blarting, mewling, snivelling. And I need to see Patrick, he will help. He can talk to me about the climate crisis or the trade deficit or how technically there is no such thing as a natural disaster. Any old boring shit will do, just to calm me down, get things in perspective. Shiv picks up the phone, which throws me at first. I can hear the sleep in her voice. Fog of ghosts. Fuck, it's late. What a prick. I'm light with Patrick . . . *yes . . . impromptu is the word . . . drinking buddy . . . anywhere open at this time . . . too old for all this . . . you've got to live, eh?* And then I stop and just tell him straight. That I think I need company, that I need to see him. I know he will come. After I put the phone down, I imagine him swinging his legs out of bed in the darkness, trying his best not to wake the girls as he leaves.

In the minutes (hours? Who knows?) before he gets here, I can feel that things are unspooling. I keep circling back, compulsive, relentless. I'm back in the car with Emma, driving past the places I grew up, except this time I manage to speak. And I say all of the things. Get them all out. Shovel out the dirt and the soil with my hands. Speak every one of my sins and spit them into the windshield. I say all of the things. Ten years of poison, twenty maybe. Fat, acidic globs of it. I try to throw up, first in the sink and then in the toilet. Making my body into different shapes, hoping it will help. But nothing comes out. Patrick arrives and sits near me until the crying and the mumbling slow down. And then he holds me and he feels rail thin under his shirt. He keeps speaking, trying to find the right words, and I am grateful for it. Grateful for him. Emma this and Emma that and maybe we should go outside and stare at the sun like a pair of old hippies.

Instead, we do what we know. We drink, Patrick talks about things, about Conor and Sophie and how there will be a massive economic crash soon and how the data shows it is inevitable this time even though he has been saying the same thing constantly since we were teenagers and it has never really happened. And then I talk and I keep talking until I can't stop it, a mad bird pecking at an egg because it is scared the baby will die with no air . . . *I had to leave the estate . . . I was turning everything bad . . . I wanted what you had . . . we're only going to fucking die . . . I never told you, but I think I went a bit mad . . . I think I loved Shiv for a while back then.* Without air the baby will die . . . *We're only going to fucking die . . . I think she might have felt the same . . . at least for a night . . . doesn't matter now . . . different life.* I can feel that I have gone too far, but I can't stop the words, as though they are being pulled out of me, up through my stomach, scratching the walls of my throat. The rage in him. That I'd never seen. The door, too heavy to slam, slowly closing behind him. Finally clicking shut and the furniture eating all of the sound.

Conor

My old man was a builder. The type to make a myth of it. The type who used to tell stories about how our family was made up of generations of men who knew how to build things. Don't trust a man who can't make things. Don't trust a man who can't look at a whole lot of nothing and know exactly how to turn it into a whole lot of something. That type of builder. These days, I think about him more often than I used to. Probably because I spend every waking hour at the site. I keep grabbing at him in my head, reminding myself of how dark his skin used to seem compared to the other grown-ups I knew, as if he were covered in a fine layer of clay and sand. And the smell of him, aftershave like wet wood, and too much of it, and the oil that he used to hold back his hair, long and slick and proud of it all his life. My old man was a builder. And when I was a kid it seemed like a good thing. Because when I looked at all the other dads, I always thought that mine was bigger somehow. Stronger. He seemed substantial and permanent, until all of a sudden he didn't.

The type to carry the dead with him. Names in faded green ink up and down his forearms, stories about being the life and soul of the party and warnings about how our family has the devil at its back. And just so many words. The words never stopped with him. *You can't put pennies on the railway tracks for ever and not expect a train crash. It's like the borders. You see, the borders here are all messed up because they have been formed and reformed over hundreds of years, conflicts and disputes, that's how* you get messed-up borders, and messed-up borders are the only borders you can trust. It's like scar tissue, would you ever trust a man whose face was covered in perfectly straight scars? . . . like he'd used a ruler? No you wouldn't is the answer to that . . . it's like a river, bending and turning, you wouldn't trust a straight river either, would you? No you fucking wouldn't is the answer to that as well. And then a river turns so much it eventually becomes a lake and then you can finally relax for a bit and just sit by the lake, you get me? I was never really sure whether I did get him or not. Or about whether that was actually how lakes got made. But it always made sense when he said it.

He went through a stage of telling me I shouldn't bother being a builder. Learn computers or become a fireman. *The building game was dying . . . noble trade gone to shit . . .* that sort of thing. But when it became clear I wasn't going to learn computers or become a fireman, he decided he'd rather have me on site with him than lying about . . . *making the house look untidy*. So that was it. Fifteen onwards I gave up school and carried bricks for money. I was useless at first, but over a year or so I built up enough strength to be useful and hold my own. Dipping my hands in the bucket of cleaning grit at the end of every day until eventually it stopped burning. I liked being around the older blokes, reaching to keep up with their jokes and gradually filling in their back stories from the fragments that flinted off over months of piss-taking and storytelling. There was one bloke who only worked during the summer, when there was plenty to do and they needed an extra pair of hands. Every summer he'd reappear, quietly laying brick after brick. He'd sit apart from everyone at lunchtimes and read from a small red Bible that he kept wrapped in a plastic supermarket bag with an elastic band around it. People took the piss, but mostly they just left him be. I asked him about the Bible once and he told me it was the type with 365 different verses in it, one for each day of the year, so it wasn't that he was being rude, it was just that lunchtime was his only chance to read on days when he was working. Bloody good bricklayer, my old man said. Weird bastard, but a bloody good bricklayer.

Eventually I went from useful to decent to good. By the time I was eighteen I could do most things on site and I had a reasonable enough eye to know whether a new lad was going to be an asset or a liability by the time they had laid a layer or two of bricks. And I liked the money. It wasn't a lot, but compared to Patrick earning sweet fuck all going to college, Oli earning sweet fuck all going absolutely nowhere and Rian slaloming about like some demented market trader, I felt rich by comparison. In the chinks, we used to say. And back then I felt like I was permanently in the chinks. By lunchtime on a Friday, the whole site would be in the pub, each with three hundred quid or so in rolled-up banknotes. It seemed like plenty; it seemed like more than enough. And it seemed to flow through us; we'd play heads or tails for twenty quid a time, and you could easily walk home with double what you had when you started drinking, or with nothing left whatsoever and with a long boring weekend spread out ahead of you. I'd act like my old man as well, saying things I didn't really mean, stretching out my stories, always reaching for the laugh or for the thing people might remember . . . *BBQ crisps are the devil's work mate . . . BBQ isn't a flavour, it's a cooking method . . . it's like having oven-flavoured crisps or microwave-flavoured crisps . . . have you noticed that the more religious people are, the more likely they are to drink Guinness? . . . body of Christ in the morning and a glass of priest in the evening . . . black smock and white collar . . . get it down you.* I don't think I've ever been as happy as I was then, never as far away from the darkness.

I think about him more these days. I suppose I miss him. Feeling him there on the site, watching something real come up out of the mud. Watching me make something. When his body broke, we just swapped mine in, seamless, no need to stop building; there is always another body to swap in when the older ones are used up. I don't want them to swap in my son when I am gone, when my blood turns black. I don't want it to keep happening. I keep telling Sophie that I won't let it happen, that I'll speak to Sean properly and not in stories and jokes and then in silence and that I won't let myself dry up or drift away. I won't ruin things by watching him too hard, by thinking that I am always about to miss something and that there is always danger. I know you can't let your heart go weird, that you can't let it become a boulder or a broken piece of brick. Let it be something clear and delicate, like water or wind or an X-ray plate that hasn't been used yet.

Shiv

You just have to treat it as a series of discrete tasks, repeated again and again until you think you have gone totally insane. That's what having a baby is. At least to begin with. Just a steady rhythm of folding things and wiping things and then putting things on and then taking off the things that you only just put on. It's people telling you that the tiny hats and tiny socks are unbearably cute but to you they are just fiddly bits of material that you spend your life putting on and taking off again. That's what it is, just an ocean of cleaning and feeding and delirium that every now and then is shot through with complete joy. You keep doing this until the ratios gradually begin to change, until the things you put on start to stay on for slightly longer and until the joy starts to come slightly more regularly. And it does.

I reckon there are two parts to happiness, the pleasure and the purpose: the things that feel nice and the things that feel meaningful. And the key is to make sure you have both, keep shifting your life to make sure you don't have too much of one and not enough of the other. Well, when you first have a kid, it is all purpose; minute to minute it feels fucking horrific, but you know deep down that something important is happening. And then one day you find yourself laughing so hard at something your kid says that you can hardly breathe, or they do something slapstick like spit out banana on a family member you don't like and everything feels O.K., the pleasure is back. You just keep pushing through, and you think you're not ready because who is ever ready and then you think maybe I am ready actually and maybe this will be O.K. and maybe there is enough of everything to go around after all.

This is what I tell Sophie when she comes around, harried and red eyed and telling me she can't do the things that need doing. I tell her precisely this and a load of other things that are basically versions of this, versions of the same point. I say them because they are the only things I know are true. They were true when Patrick and I had Molly, and they were true all over again a year later when Freya came along. I can tell that she is bone tired, that type of tired where you start to see shadows moving in the corners of your vision and begin to wonder if people who believe in ghosts are mostly just people who are really really tired. I also say these things to her because they are the only things I really have to give to her, other than a few hours of adult company and a change of scenery, a different sofa to sit and be tired on. Somebody to drink wine with, or someone to convince you that it is probably a bit early for wine and that if we've got things to be doing later in the day then maybe we should have coffee instead. And it sort of works, I think. It sort of helps. I watch her gently lower Sean onto a mat in the corner of the room, surprised somehow by how delicate and loving she is, how gentle. He's a tiny thing, thick strip of dark hair down the centre of his head. I let my girls coo over him, pulling faces at him and asking us questions like . . . *can he see me? . . . does he know who I am? . . . would it be weird to put his whole hand in my mouth? . . . I think it would fit!* It's strange that my girls are already looking at the baby as if he's an alien, something they couldn't imagine being. I want to tell them that it was only yesterday that they were that small, and that I know it seems crazy but being a baby comes back again eventually. You start to want things so much that you feel like screaming until someone gives them to you, you start to want someone to wrap you up so tight that your arms don't move, you want to stop saying words and just make sounds instead, you want to sleep all of the time or never at all. I want to tell them that it all comes back.

In this state, exactly as she is this second, exhausted and wrung out, Sophie doesn't want to hear any of the things I have to say to her. And I get that. I really get that. But it's a risk, I want to tell her, it's a risk being the way she is for too long. You can lose track of how to get back to normal, and before you know it something in you has curdled and gone off and nothing feels right any more. When she finally speaks, loosened by wine, it all comes out at once, frantic and surreal. She says she doesn't know what the fuck she was thinking with Conor . . . that she's started to hate his hands on her . . . that sometimes he scares her . . . that something must be rotting inside him because his breath always smells weird to her, as if he hasn't brushed his teeth even when she knows he has . . . that she can't kiss him because his spit has turned too thick.

I let her talk because she obviously needs to, and I try my best to follow, but she is going too deep, too fast. Something is really off, that much is clear, but she either doesn't have the right words for it or doesn't want to name it. So I try to be practical, to warn her against letting things take on their own momentum. I tell her you can't just let the tailspin happen. That you'll hit the ground and then you'll be on fire and then you'll be fucked. That's how that story ends. I tell her we can't just curse the future, going around reading bones and tea leaves and saying everything is about to turn bad. Because doing that is the quickest way to ensure that they actually do. I tell her that sometimes it is best to just pretend everything is O.K. for a bit until things actually feel O.K. and then eventually you can stop pretending. I tell her I know it's not very romantic, but fuck it, it's what has got Patrick and me through all of these years. A few close calls, but it always turned out alright in the end. Just ride the wave. I tell her that Patrick and I aren't even talking at the minute . . . *fuck knows why. He came back one night and the words had just stopped . . . but it's fine, let him be silent, it's always nothing, in a few days things will be back to normal . . . they always are. You have to assume you're going to make it . . . assume things are O.K.* And I believe it too. I believe every word. You have to let the glass empty, let the glass refill, but never stop drinking from it, that's the important thing. Bend at the elbow, Sophie, breathe, try to get some fucking sleep.

Patrick

The hotel room door didn't even slam. I could feel my fingers gripping its edges and the flash of fear that I might have pulled it shut so hard that I'd trap them in the door. But the hotel room door didn't even slam. The mechanism caught, silently, and then the door edged its way slowly and evenly back into its frame, like something extremely light falling extremely gently onto something extremely soft. I remembered Rian's city flat, where the cupboards and drawers did the same. Add it to the list of fucking pointless things that rich people spend their money on, doors that close incredibly slowly. I had to leave; I couldn't stand to be in that room with him for a second longer, hearing him talk and talk and talk as if he might never stop talking. Talking as if talking was always the right thing and as if talking always helped. As if talking wasn't sometimes a tyranny all of its own. I've always hated that, the compulsion to talk things out, as though everything that exists has a word for it and everything that can be said should be said. It's the same as when people say that everything has an opposite, when really hardly anything does. Pleasure and pain, fine, night and day, fine, but what's the opposite of a table or an astronaut or a daffodil or a bowl of cereal? Most things don't have opposites and most things that matter don't have words at all. I wish we settled more things with silence, or with bodies, with fucking or fighting. Just no more talking. Sometimes there is just no room left for more words.

But Rian wouldn't stop. I couldn't stand him telling me

those things, slurring them at me as though he were giving me a gift, another one of his presents sent from Tokyo or Geneva or Munich. He could have just not spoken. Those words weren't for me, they were for him. What did he think I could possibly want with them, with the thought of him lying all of these years, with the thought of his hands on Shiv, or hers on him. Those words weren't for me, he just didn't want them in him any more, he needed to fetch them up off his lungs. It's like telling somebody you once pissed in their coffee, years after they have finished drinking it; who the fuck does that help? Certainly not the person who drank the piss. And there I was, minutes before, rubbing his back through his expensive shirt and telling him to come outside and maybe get some fresh air. Suggesting we watch the fucking sun come up. Enough words. I couldn't stand to be there for another second. The hotel door didn't even slam.

The sun is actually coming up now, catching the glass of the lobby door as I leave and lighting up the metal railing where I locked up my bike a few hours earlier. It's one of those rare times when I am actually grateful for the bike, for the lightness of it under my body, the way it makes me feel the imperfections and cracks in the road that I would never have noticed otherwise, and for the way it makes places seem smaller, closer together, more knowable. The roads are still empty; it will be an hour or more before they start to come alive with cars and buses, before the day starts to grow a new skin. I cycle fast, tipping my head back and gulping down pint after pint of morning air, like if I get enough of it down me, it will quiet Rian's voice, which is currently smashing against the inside of my skull. Fuck this, fuck him. Fuck the sounds and the pictures. And fuck the stupid things too, the male pride and the questions and the details and the who knew and the how many times. Fuck the way new light casts itself backwards and starts to discolour everything, like a photo being bleached by the sun until you can't recognise the faces. And fuck the what were they thinking and the what has been happening all of these years and all the times he was in my home and the what other secrets are there and the am I the cunt here. And fuck making me think these things when I know I've no right to. When deep down I know it doesn't matter. But I can't make myself be reasonable. I feel like something has been taken from me, and I also feel like a complete bastard for feeling like something has been taken from me. It's that old gypsy phrase, stealing from someone is taking a bit of the light that god gave them. And I know it's stupid, but that's what it feels like. As if someone has taken some of the light.

Shiv is still asleep when I lean my bike against the wall in the hallway and slide back into bed without taking my clothes off. My eyes are locked on the ceiling, trying to talk myself down. I can feel the effects of the drink and the morning air, there's a pulsing in my temples and the urge to wake her keeps rising up in me. I want to shake her awake, make her speak to me. I can't stand the curve of her back, and her voice locked in her chest while she sleeps. Maybe if I shake her awake it will dislodge the words and she'll open her eyes and immediately say the perfect thing, a prayer or a spell or a Hail Mary, and all the wrong things will fall away and all the right things will come rushing back into the room. But I don't do it, there really have been enough words tonight. No more words tonight, not a single one. And tomorrow as well, there will be as much silence as I can get away with. No talking and don't be a prick. That's the plan. Don't imagine their hands or their bodies. Bury the thoughts in silence. Wait for the world to jolt me back. Don't wake her, try to sleep, just for an hour or so.

But the sleep doesn't come. And the silence isn't nearly enough to bury the thoughts. And I can't shake their bodies and their hands and their shapes. The morning is fully here now, white light under the curtains, blistering the carpet and slowly creeping up the bedroom wall. I check my phone: no messages, no missed calls. In an hour the alarm will go off, and half an hour after that the girls will be awake and the flat will be full of sound. The high, clear, beautiful sound of them. Most of all I want to shake this and then fix this and then forget this. But all I can think to do is be quiet. I turn off the alarm. An hour of sleep is worse than no sleep at all. As I am about to leave the room Shiv stirs . . . *is it time to wake up already?* I don't answer her, let her roll over and go straight back to sleep. I couldn't even say . . . *no, not yet, go back to sleep for another hour.* I couldn't even say that. All I can think to do is be quiet.

Shiv

Four days is quite a long time, even for Patrick. I'm used to a day or so of silence, once or twice a year. But then the ice melts or the dam breaks or the cloud bursts or whatever the right water metaphor is. The point is that the words always come pouring back in eventually. I used to hate the silences, but as time has gone on I've got accustomed to it, to the point that I've started to not mind it at all. My life is loud. A bit of a break from the same voice I've been hearing every single day for decades isn't actually such a bad thing. It might even be healthy.

But this is the fourth day, the longest it has ever been. And I don't like that at all. Four days is too much heaviness, and the girls have started to notice that we aren't talking. Patrick is handing out bowls of cereal, plastic cups of orange juice, manoeuvring himself around the kitchen in counterintuitive patterns so he doesn't have to look me directly in the face. He can be such a baby sometimes. Enough of this. I corner him, throw my arms out wide so that he can't get past me . . . *are you trying to break some sort of record?* . . . *did someone cut out your tongue?* . . . *shall I get you a stick so you can write your answer in the mud?* No response. Dickhead.

He has always been a bit like this, a bit prone to silences, even when we were kids. For a while I thought he was just doing the whole moody, thoughtful outsider thing and that he'd grow out of it eventually. But he never really did, it just sort of stuck. And even now, even when he's not doing it deliberately, it can be a real feast and famine situation. Patrick can be the quietest person on a night out and then something somebody says will ignite him and the sentences come rolling out of him. And you know they've been brewing for ages because they come out in reams, like fully formed paragraphs. I love to see him in full flow like that, and I love to see other people see it for the first time. I like to watch people watch him, watch them see a bit of his inner world, just for a minute or two, see a slice of what I love so much. The anger and the vision and the ability to see how absurd and funny things are, even when they are bleak as fuck, which in Patrick's view they almost always are. But still, four days is too much. Enough now.

Four days starts to affect the flow of things. A life like ours, decades in the making, ends up amassing hundreds of tedious but necessary questions. Questions that need to be constantly asked and answered and then re-asked and re-answered, on an endless loop, with only the slightest variations. But the variations matter. Who is doing what when, who is picking this thing up from that place, who has spoken to that person and who has filled in that form that we both agreed one of us needed to fill in. It all adds up, it's the texture of things, and you can't negotiate it properly if one of you has taken a four-day vow of silence. Something will give, something will go wrong. It can feel like those things are just administrative, but they are not, they are more than that, and you have to get them right. Add them all together and they make up so much of a life together. Iron them out, make them run on rails, make them so easy they become invisible, fuck, make them graceful, make a fucking ballet out of who is going to the shop if you have to. But they need to work, otherwise things just get too hard, too quickly.

But there are no words when I throw my arms out wide and block his way, and no smile when I ask him if he wants a stick to scratch a message in the mud. Instead, he flinches away from me when I put my hand on his shoulder and try to draw him in for a hug. Usually, if I take the piss a bit, lighten things, he'll start to relent and open up, a laugh at first and then a fuck you and then finally whatever it is gets dropped. But today it doesn't work, he just closes up even more, and then walks straight past me and into the hallway. I watch him kneel down next to his bike, pressing his fingers quickly against the tyres to check they are firm enough and then clipping his phone onto the holder in the centre of the handlebars.

It's strange to see how light and easy he is with the bike these days. When he first had it, he seemed to be always yanking and pulling it, calling it a cunt under his breath. And we'd hear it periodically crash to the floor because he hadn't leaned it against the wall at the right angle. I watch him leave the flat and then I move to the window and watch him leave the tower block, pushing the bike for a few yards while he messes with his headphones. Once he starts riding he is out of sight in seconds, overtaking the cars that have already started to fill the roads and slow one another down.

Most days, by the time the girls are at school and I've tried to deal with some of the chaos they've left in their wake, with the half-eaten breakfast and the clothes on the stairs and the last bit of soap snapped into unusable pieces and left in the sink, it only feels like a few minutes before Patrick is back to eat lunch. But today feels longer; carrying his silence with me is making the hours drag, heavy and slow. To kill an hour I walk over to the park, with its man-made lake, full of swans and geese, beer cans and glass bottles and those plastic lifesaver rings that kids can't resist throwing into the water. Not that I blame them; we were the same. Every time I'm here I remember when Patrick did it, swung too hard and ended up slipping over, plunging one of his legs into the brown water, fresh trainers and all. The sight of it was funny enough, but then one of the geese made a sound that we all swore to god sounded like laughter. The bastard geese were laughing at him. Me, Oli, Rian, Conor, we all laughed until our sides hurt, until Patrick had no choice but to join in. The type of laughter that made you want to say words like helpless and doubled-up. People falling over is funny, people falling over in dirty water is funnier, and people falling over in dirty water while a goose laughs at them is even funnier still. *Molly, Freya . . . when we were little, your daddy fell in the water and one of those big ducks laughed at him . . . silly Daddy.*

By the time Patrick arrives back for lunch, I know he will only have time to eat and then leave, if he wants to make sure he catches the tail end of the busy period. But he'll have to stay until he talks, until he tells me what's wrong. I don't care about the lunchtime rush, not today. At first, nothing comes, and then I push some more and nothing comes again. Until finally he speaks, and I can't believe what he is saying . . . *I can't get it out of my head . . . I can't fucking believe it . . . you two, together, like that . . . your hands . . . fuck, I can barely speak . . . you're going to need to answer all of the questions I ask you . . . even if you don't think they're fair . . . fuck, I'm not sure I can do this.* And on it goes, and the words don't stop.

Patrick

Sometimes you have to ask permission to be a prick. Allow me to be this way, please, I promise I'd only ask if I absolutely had to. There's something I need to get over, or get past. It's like that old blues song . . . *I got stones in my passway, and my road seems dark as night.* If you'll just let me be a prick for a second, then we can clear the fucking stones. I remember reading somewhere that maybe that song is actually about impotence, but it doesn't matter really; it makes sense either way. There's no way forward here until we clear the road. And ever since that night with Rian, there have been stones in my passway, fuck, there have been stones in my stomach, heavy and inert and unmoving, grinding against my insides. So just let me be a prick. I know this is unfair. But I can't shake the image of it, of you. Of you and him. Do you remember that time in the Trident, when that old lad was so pissed that he threw up into his pint glass, but he was that out of it that he just drank the vomit as if nothing had happened, and then threw up again straight after, refilling his pint glass with bile and stomach acid? Well that's how this fucking feels, a disgusting loop. Ouroboric. A snake eating itself and then vomiting bits of itself into a pint glass. I've tried everything, but nothing has worked. I even tried the idea that maybe it might turn me on, imagining you opening yourself to someone new, imagining the strangeness of it. But it didn't turn me on. It made me lose my hard-on in the shower. Stones in my passway. Stones in my stomach. Stones in my pockets and me in the lake if you won't just let me say what I need to say.

I might have been willing to wait a few more days, until it felt a bit less raw. I thought that if I could find my way through it on my own, or at least find my way through some of it on my own, there would be less chance I'd say something truly poisonous, something we would both struggle to forget. But Shiv wasn't going to let that happen, she was going to pull the words out of me whether I liked it or not. I'd felt her trying that morning, but I'd ignored it, pushed past her and out of the flat. I needed a few more hours where I didn't have to summon it up and make it real. I knew Shiv would speak it into existence and make it undeniable. A few more hours of it being formless and disembodied. I didn't want to press my hand against the ghosts and feel the throb of something living pressing back against me. So I waited as long as I could. I waited until there wasn't any other option but to start speaking.

And when it came to it, I had to ask for every single thing that I knew deep down I shouldn't want or need. *First, can you not touch me, please, just for a minute. And can you just let me be a prick, don't point it out to me, I know full well how I am being.* So I just keep asking, like a spoiled kid who is suddenly interested in their old toys as soon as they see them in some other kid's hand . . . *how many times (once) . . . Once? (well, one night) . . . where the fuck was I? (away) thank fuck . . . anything since? (no) . . . thank fuck . . . is that why Rian went away to begin with? (no idea) . . . do you ever think of him? (no) . . . not once? (of course, but only with regret, actually no, not just regret, just in the way everyone thinks about things that they have done all of the time, it's a stupid question) . . . do you wish you were with him instead of me? (don't be fucking ridiculous, don't ask me that) . . . did you enjoy it? (enjoy is not the right word, feelings about it were messy) . . . do you ever think about him while we fuck? (never) . . . do you ever think about him when you touch yourself? (no) . . . but have you ever? (hesitant no) . . . will we be*

O.K.? *(yes, we will be O.K.)* . . . *do you promise we will be O.K.?* *(yes, I promise we will be O.K.).*

And I do know that Shiv is right, that we will be O.K. It's just that it feels delicate right this second. Delicate like when you slide a jumper over your body after a fight or a fall and the cotton brushes against the deep purple of your bruises and the black and red of your cuts. Like how every time the material touches your skin you can feel the fists or the pavement against your body all over again. Except the next time you pull the jumper on you feel it a tiny bit less and the time after that you feel it a tiny bit less again until eventually there isn't much of a memory at all, and the fists and the pavement fall away so much that you forget they were ever real. It's the same pattern when somebody you love dies. The pain never goes; it just gets progressively more spaced out. In the beginning it is there every second of every day, as if the air is made up of their absence. And then after a while it is not every second, it is just every minute, and then every hour and eventually just on anniversaries or when you hear a particular accent or a particular phrase or song. The sadness never goes away, it just gets so spaced out that you can carry on living as though it has. It's all the same. It's all just time. Fuck, I mean, even mountains are growing and shrinking and dying, we just don't live long enough or watch closely enough to ever notice. Maybe we might notice a city dying, or changing, or being reborn, getting bigger and taller, or shrinking away because of neglect. But even that is hard to imagine sometimes. Hard to look at where you live, and the people in it, its noises and smells and rituals and think . . . soon enough none of this will be here. In the end it's all just time, and making and breaking and bruises and healing.

In bed that night, Shiv and I found each other, her hands reaching over and pulling me on top of her. There was something desperate and alive and hurried about it. Afterwards I turned my head away so Shiv didn't have to see me trying to fold my anger small enough that we could hide it somewhere we'd forget. Hard to sleep and a heavy thrum against my ribs all night. Thoughts that wouldn't go quiet . . . there was something sharp and cold about Rian telling me what he did . . . he'll have to stay away, for a bit at least . . . while we fix this . . . if I close my eyes I'll have that dream again where something is tearing after me and my legs won't move properly so I have to just give in . . . I need a different job . . . when I was a kid I was sure that god wanted me to be a priest or a preacher or a pope . . . it never rains in bad dreams . . . why does some light make snow look blue? . . . this will be fine . . . give it time . . . one foot in front of the other.

Shiv

The thing is, I'd known. I'd known it would hurt Patrick if I let something happen between me and Rian, but I did it anyway. Anyone who has known pain knows it hurts less if you invite it in yourself, if you control when it is going to arrive rather than waiting for the universe to land it on your doorstep when you are not expecting it. It sounds stupid, but that's what I did, I think. I knew I was summoning something painful into our lives, but better that than to sit there helpless, waiting for another wave to crash against the side of us. We'd already been going through a lot at the time, feeling fragile and haunted. Looking back now, it's as though I lost patience and just decided we all had to get to know the dead.

Because those months Patrick was away at university were fucking horrible. A lifetime ago now, but still so easy to summon. It was as if I was living in a house I didn't know. Sleeping in a bed I didn't know. I did nothing, just waited for him. Drank, smoked cheap weed, waited. Drank, smoked cheap weed, waited. I remember feeling as if time had slowed down. As if my life was passing incredibly slowly but everybody else's was passing at normal speed. I'd look out of the window and the people seemed to be moving so fast. I wondered how they had the energy. Maybe they only moved when I was looking at them? Maybe once they closed their front doors they just sat there in the darkness, utterly still, recharging all night so they could run past my window again the next day. I was sad. Extremely sad. And lonely.

I knew what would happen if I called Rian. I knew what would happen and I did it anyway. I can remember walking over there, knowing that if I touched Rian, if I let him know it was O.K., he would give in straight away. I knew it had hurt him to see me with Patrick over the years, that maybe there had been times he thought it should have been him. He'd never said a word, he'd never acted, but there were enough heavy looks and enough early exits for me to know. It sounds awful to say now, but I remember being excited on my way there, by the risk of it, by my power. I was soaking wet before I even knocked on the door. I asked if I could stay with him. Told him I couldn't spend any more time by myself. His strange hand on me, a new hand. And that night I was greedy for him; I couldn't leave him alone. We kept reaching for one another in the darkness, half-asleep, me pulling him inside me over and over again. I knew it would only happen once, that this was all there would be. We both did, I think. That was the only way it could happen. Walking home the next day, I'd expected to feel awful, to feel sick with guilt, but I didn't. It felt fine. I still missed Patrick, I still knew that a life with him was what I had chosen and I still knew that it was the right choice.

It was odd between Rian and me for a few months after, but not for long. We both knew it was a one-off, something kind and generous we had given to each other when we both needed it. We hadn't spoken about it since, and I was grateful to him for that. It's just something we shared. Something we guarded and watched over. Every so often it felt like something ancient and vital, a religious relic or something. But mostly, it didn't feel like that at all. Mostly it felt like something that didn't really matter, like an urn with somebody else's dead pet in it, or a gaudy commemorative fifty pence piece. Mostly, it was fine.

Until now. It was fine until Rian decided he had the right to reach into the wound and try to unpick the stitches. And for what? Because his life had slipped out of focus over the past couple of years? Because he'd drifted too far from home and started to feel fucking sentimental about his choices? As though his choices were uniquely fraught, uniquely contorting and sad and full of compromise? It's hard not to hate the arrogance of that, of the idea that we haven't all had to shape what we have out of a mixture of regrets and maybes and almosts and a handful of whatever is good that we manage to find lying around in the meantime.

But Rian can't be the focus. I know how to protect things when they feel like they might be at risk of breaking. You close ranks. You focus on the small, repeatable actions. You hold onto the guardrails until you re-establish the rhythm of things. The melody can come later. Forgiveness, happiness, new joy, that can all come later. When things feel like they might be breaking it is only the rhythm that matters. The steady beat of the everyday. Patrick can decide what happens between him and Rian, if there's enough left between them at this point to make it worth saving. I hope there is, but if it really came to it, I'd cut the rope myself and let him float away from our lives. There are times when you have to pull the people closest to you even closer still. So for now, that's what I'll do. I'll let Patrick ask his questions and speak his demons until he has cleared enough bile from his stomach to let something purer start coming through. And I'll reach for his body as well, for its familiar shape and its familiar smell. His body, now. As it is. Alive and finding its footing, finding its grip. Finding its way back.

Conor

Sophie has gone. Taken Sean and driven up the motorway to her parents' house, filling up their house and leaving ours empty. So quiet. So unbelievably quiet. I'd always imagined it full of noise, all of the boring noise a family makes. All of the *should we get insurance or should we not bother?* and *is there something wrong with the extractor fan?* and *maybe we should just move . . . this whole place feels like it is falling to bits.* None of that now. Just the silence.

It's been coming for a while. Over the last few months, it had got so bad between us that I was making sure I was gone before Sophie woke up. It had got to the point where I couldn't stand the way she looked at me in the morning, her eyes full of it as soon as they opened. It would start as something like shock or disgust, an instinctive recoiling from the fact that I was there, in her bed. And then as the minutes went by the disgust would harden, first into fury and then quickly into coldness. I'd watch her shutting down, switching off behind the eyes and turning on a different switch, one that made every movement seem distant and rehearsed. When this happened I would focus on the mole just above her lip, on the left-hand side. It helped me hold my nerve, my own anger, and gave me something to concentrate on that wasn't her eyes, her disdain. I couldn't bear it. I preferred the way she was before the silence started, when she was all bile and fuck you and you're a failure and I hate you. And there had been moments when she had come at me, swinging punches, clawing and biting at my skin. And I had preferred that too. I would hold her arms by her side to try to calm things and I'd think that at least the anger was open, at least the anger was opening things up. Maybe the anger would break something, melt something, and then there would be space for all of this to take root in her and grow. Some room in her for a picture of us as a family, as something new but worth protecting.

But even the anger had stopped; there were no more spaces being torn open. So I'd sneak out of the room as soon as I woke up, look in on Sean, click the front door and then stay out at the site until it was late enough that Sophie might have gone to bed. Or at the very least late enough that she would have gone upstairs so I could just carry on drinking until I heard that she had stopped moving about. Pathetic really. To let things get this messed up at the exact time that things were supposed to be getting better. Self-pity doesn't help, but it comes in waves anyway. What have I killed with my wanting and my need, what have I broken with my ugly hands?

I'd got too greedy, too desperate. I'd fucked it up and Sophie knew it. The site is badly over leveraged, too many short-term fixes to cover my back and all of them starting to be called in before I have enough on hand to pay them. I didn't want to tell Rian; I was sure I could turn it around, but the only way I could buy any time was to borrow against the house, the only thing we had of any value. I should have waited to tell Sophie, not let it slip out when I had sloped in at midnight, more than half cut and feeling like I didn't have much else left to lose. The argument spun us all round the house, from the bedroom, downstairs and then settling in the kitchen. Sophie saying she'd had enough of me, spitting her words, like her lungs contained all the sickness of the world and she needed it out of her body. And then, finally, the blankness. Giving into it the way I used to so easily when I was a kid. Nothing but the pulse of it, passing through my hands as they met the edge of her jaw, once, twice; nothing but my feet as they met the cave of her chest. She crawled away from me. The distant sound of her voice, trying to fight its way through the haze, and then the sound of her feet on the stairs. The door slamming shut, the car starting, a dial tone ringing out, an umbrella in the corner, turned out like a cracked ribcage.

That's how the ritual started, a new plan scratched out in the mud and the dust. I come to the site every day, seven days a week, and haven't missed a day in months. The site feels like something permanent. Something changing, but something permanent. Everything else is fucking up and going to shit and falling to pieces, so it's good to be around something that at least feels like it is doing what it is supposed to be doing, growing, progressing, minute by minute getting slightly more real and slightly more useful. For now at least. And it's the right time of year for it. Long, light days, the sun skittering up the steel and the scaffold and then fanning out across the wooden crossbeams. I've learned which parts of the metal will get too hot to touch and for how long and at what point they will be just warm enough to curl your hands around and let some of the heat transfer to your skin. If nobody is in your eyeline, you can even lean right in and press your face against the warmth, hold it there against your cheek and your eye-socket for a few seconds. I'm sure that I'm not the only one who does that.

I turn up early these days. Really early. I like to circle the perimeter of the site as many times as I can before the rest of the lads start arriving. It reminds me of those first days after Sophie and Sean got back from the hospital, walking him round and round the estate for hours to try to give her some space to sleep. I've got into the habit of trying to loop around the site at least ten times if possible. The downside is that I can end up feeling on edge for the rest of the day if I don't make it all the way around the site enough times. Once I have though, something in me unwinds and I can just wait for the sounds of cars pulling up, radios shutting off mid song as the keys get pulled out, or Oli's voice, loud as it ever was but steadier these days, brighter somehow. And as the hours pass, the light will pick a new patch, hour by hour, sliding up bricks and buildings and marking the time until they all go home and the site is soaked in silence again. It's the only way I've found to mark the time, by just giving myself over to the pulse and the ebb of it. Some days something new will have sprung up by the time everyone clocks off, the outline of a new building, incomplete, as if someone has drawn it from memory. And other days there is nothing new to see, but I know what is there has still changed, been made stronger, filled in, shaded between the lines. And then, when everyone has finally left, when I have turned down the final offer of the pub and the pints and jokes and the gripes, I start my walk again. Ten times around the perimeter and then I can stop. I sit on the wall nearest to the entrance, open the vodka I keep in my work bag and let the clear medicinal burn slide down my throat over and over until there is too much darkness or too much cold to stay for a minute longer. Then I'll leave. Only then. That is the new ritual.

And the ritual gets bigger, expands to fill the spaces. When I get back from the site, I just carry on walking, but this time around the rooms of the house. Some sort of lunatic vigil, tracing memory lines from room to room, feeling the different types of silence that each of the spaces makes. With no eyes on me, with nobody waking me in the middle of the night, I have just started to drink until the blackness comes. I wake slumped against the kitchen wall, or in the hallway or on the stairs, full of bruises and carpet burns, an outbox of hundreds of messages and unanswered calls and the soupy memory of having left desperate voicemails. Nights of pleading and threatening and apologising and then finally of pulling myself into the morning, into another day where I might seek out the first sun on the bricks and press my face against the warm heat of the metal. Drive out towards the site, past the lake we used to mess about on when we were kids, the way it wets the morning air and the cans that people leave around the fringe of it. Always vodka, because it doesn't come out in your sweat, doesn't have that sweet mulch smell, just clear and mineral and astringent. And I swear we never used to leave our cans around the lake like that. And there are droplets hanging from the steel this morning, and I wonder if the weather is starting to turn, and I wonder where I got the stupid idea that some things are supposed to last a long time.

Rian

The sleep in my new house is different. Dense. It clings to me for hours, leaves a film on my skin that lasts half the day. It makes me wonder if maybe I hadn't slept properly at all since I left. A decade of snatched hours, short and shallow and dreamless, did any of that really count, did any of it do whatever it is that sleep is supposed to do? Here, on the edge of the estate, the dreams are full of real things, streets and people, boats and rocks and trees and water. And for the last week, the same bird has turned up every night, a magpie with a dark green stripe down its back.

After I wake, it takes a few seconds to remember where I am, and then a few seconds more to remember what I have done. A few seconds and then the stuff with Patrick will come roaring back, pushing its way through the haze and making me wince and shiver, pressing my head back against my pillow in the hope of driving out the memory of that night. Feeling the shame of it in every single one of my bones. I've had to stay away a bit since that night, despite being desperate to see Patrick and apologise, throw myself on his mercy and ask what I need to say or do to make things normal again. And I want to be around Shiv and the girls too, let some of the good stuff rub off on me. But not for now, not yet. I shouldn't have said what I said, but it didn't feel like a choice at the time. Most important things aren't really choices, not really, not in any way that matters. I didn't choose it; it just came pouring out. It came out like a purge, an exorcism. And something in me let it happen, as if it might get rid of all of the blackness and the envy. It came pouring out as penance for all of the times that I've fucked up and for all of the people I should have loved properly but didn't.

The shame of it stays until I manage to shake myself out of bed. So I'm learning to do that as quickly as possible, no dwelling. Like my old man used to say, don't piss in your own bathwater and then expect it to clean you. Once I am up, the other thing hovers into view: what the hell do you do with a life when you don't have to do anything at all? I came home, that's one thing, but then what? I got this house on the edge of the estate, but then what? I suppose I just live in it, until I die in it, and that is more or less what a life is? There would be worse places to do it, I suppose. The house is near where we used to go to school, but the school isn't there any more. A newer one has opened a few miles away and where the old one used to be there is a supermarket and a shop that sells cheap sportswear and trainers. At some point I'll have to make this house nicer, if I'm going to stay here. It's big enough, but it is fucking ugly, full of bad colours and bad choices. It looks the same way I imagine it looked thirty years ago, and I imagine that it probably looked quite shit even then. I'll get someone who knows about furniture and paint and design to come in and sort it all out. I don't want to choose how it looks; I care about not having to choose furniture way more than I care about furniture. As long as it doesn't look like one of those generic members' clubs I've wasted so much time in over the past few years. Those places are always full of cracked leather, dark greens and reds, browning at the edges. None of that. I'm done with making things seem older than they really are or more broken than they really are. No more of that.

One of the things I do with my life, in the absence of any better ideas, is drink loads of coffee. Buckets. Every morning now, I pad downstairs, brew up a pot and then sit and slowly drink the whole thing until I am vibrating with dirty energy. And then

I walk. I'll walk for hours and hours, relearning the place, letting it seep back into me. I'll walk to the old lake, round it a few times, think about the time Patrick fell in there and a goose laughed at him. A goose literally laughed at him. Amazing. And then up past the place where the library used to be, the one Patrick started randomly asking about out of nowhere. I keep thinking I'll see him on his bike while I'm out walking, but I haven't yet. I've seen a few others doing it, same uniform, indistinguishable from a distance, but a world away up close. Weird to think of Patrick in a uniform at all, to be honest. When we were kids he'd always be the one writing things in biro along the white edges of his trainers or in marker pen down the straps of his backpack. Determined to stand out.

I've been trying to dry out a bit as well, let some of the drink drain away. Walking at night helps, wears me out, helps me sleep without needing to open a bottle. A few nights ago, I saw Conor while I was out walking. He was pacing around the edge of the site, phone against his ear and swaying from side to side. I thought about going over but I got the sense he wouldn't be in the mood to talk and would be embarrassed for me to see him so messed up now that he sort of works for me. By the time I got home that night, it was sheeting with rain. I wondered if he was still out there. He probably was, the mad bastard. I messaged him before I fell asleep . . . *walked past the site today, looking great, don't work too hard or you'll make me feel like a prick. Night mate x*

And I listen to music. I properly listen. For a long time I couldn't listen, years maybe, not properly. But since I came back I can't get enough of it. I want thunders of sound and strange lyrics that feel like they are braided up in grass and vine and the type of rolling piano loops that used to make us euphoric twenty years ago. Some nights I ask Oli to come over and listen to records with me. I know that if he replies he's having a good day, a clean day; he's stopped letting me see him when he's messed up, which seems like a good sign. The nights he comes round he'll smash through the silence of the house with his gleeful jabber, a million miles an hour, always too loud and always too fast. I try to talk to him, about the weight of things, about whether he ever wondered if we'd all have to watch each other get old one day. But he'll cut right through it, telling me to perk up, to buy a fucking dog . . . *or maybe even a rabbit . . . rabbits are more fun than you think . . . have you heard this . . . you'll love this . . . pick the mood up . . . big tune.* He'll still be changing tracks every few minutes even as I can feel myself falling asleep on the sofa. Low electronic shimmers in my dreams and Oli gone by the time I wake up. And then another day. What do you do with a life? If I wait long enough, then it will come to me. You can't force it. You can't go around trying to make the world answer you, having conversations with the sky or the sea. None of that.

Oli

It's a bit by bit, day by day, inch by inch thing. But I'm getting better, something is lifting. It started with me making promises to myself: I won't use this month, or I won't use this week, I'll go to a group, I'll get a sponsor. But I've never been that good at keeping promises, and the groups felt too much like church, so that system didn't work really, or at all, to be honest. Instead, I have to let the question fill me up, let it occupy every second if it needs to. Just answering the same question over and over again, relentlessly. Answering no. Answering no to the question: would you like something that makes you feel really really really good?

So that's what I try to do. I allow the question in and then I spend my time trying to get better at giving the right answer. Some people say there's a type of pleasure to be had in saying no to things you really want. The thrill of refusal or self-denial. But I haven't managed to find that yet, so I'm starting to wonder if that might just be some religious bollocks. To keep getting better at saying no I had to stop selling. Entirely. Not a bit on the side here and there when I was short, I had to stop entirely. You can't have it around you all the time, packaged up and ready, and the sweet, acrid smell of it on your fingers. And the worst is the excitement of the people buying it from you, the need in their eyes as they hand over the crumpled tenners as quickly as they can. It transmits. Comes straight off them and straight into me, an electric current passing through copper. Not like those circuit diagrams we had to draw at school, four clean straight lines and neat symbols for the battery and the bulb. More like you find in an old house, a mess of exposed wires, knotted up and installed by someone who didn't know what they were doing.

And that's as close as I have to a plan; stop selling and keep getting gradually better at saying no. Tell myself I don't want it until I start to lose track of whether, deep down, I actually do or not. At the minute I say yes about twice a week, and on those nights I give in completely. To the smell, the small acts of preparation, to the feel of the needle in my skin and then to the total, utter falling away. And fuck me, to the warmth of it. People always go on about how good it feels, but they never say how unbelievably warm it is. It's like being deep inside a woman, your face pressed into her neck, the smell of her skin filling up every part of you, and then somehow, as you move together, everything starting to get so warm that you both start breaking apart, becoming a million things with a million hands until the only thing left is warmth, nothing else, nothing, just the warmth. There isn't another feeling like it, and there won't be, ever. When I'm finally able to start saying no all the time, this feeling will be lost and gone and I'll miss it for the rest of my life; I might as well just accept that.

The times when I give in are getting rarer, but when they do come, they take me out for whole days. I can't work the next morning, I need to lie around and let the heat drain out of me. Conor lets me, knows if I don't turn up it is because I can't, not because I don't want to. It's incredible how patient he is with me; I'll never forget that, ever. There aren't many people who would put up with me, but he always does and always has. Never blinks. Rian too. I know it was his idea for Conor to give me the work to start with, even though he has never mentioned it or taken credit. I won't let either of them down; I'll keep getting better at answering the question. And overall, I am, overall, it's working. I can feel my energy starting to come back, my body starting to work a bit better. I've grown a small, round, hard belly and there have been a few mornings recently when I've woken up and my cock has been hard, glazed with wetness on the tip. I'm ageing backwards. And getting more useful on the site, too. I'm more and more drawn to the work, to the making. That place is like a magnet these days, or a monolith or something. It turns up in my dreams. I wonder if it does for the other lads on the site as well? Or even for the old lads who are always moaning about it. Do they all see it? The new metal and the new bricks and the clouds of chalk and dust? There's something ancient about it, humming and growing, pulling us all in. There are some nights when I dream it has burned down, that it is nothing but cinders and blackness. In that dream we all go to watch the embers, dipping our fingers in the ash and marking one another's forehead like we used to have to do at Easter. That one leaves me feeling weird for hours after I wake up, eager to get to work and see that the place is still intact, still growing and still alive.

I tell you what doesn't help the weird dreams. The fact that Conor has started walking around the site in the middle of the night. Round and round on a loop like some sort of drunk shaman. Maybe the cheeky bastard is putting a spell on us or something, to make us work harder. I've seen him a few times now, and it looks fucking eerie. Or maybe weird. I always forget which one of those is which. Eerie is when something is missing I think, and weird is when something is there that shouldn't be there. Either way, Conor walking around the site manages to feel like both of those things at once. I thought about going over the last time I saw him, but maybe it's just how he clears his head. No shame in that. None at all. I get it.

Nights are the hardest: nothing to do with my hands and not enough concentration to do much of anything. Same few pages of the paper over and over again with nothing going in, flicking through the TV and getting bored in minutes. So I've started to see Rian whenever I can. Still can't quite believe he is back. Out of nowhere one day, back. To sort his head out he says. Mad. This isn't the place to sort your head out. If I had his money I'd be off, out, you wouldn't see me for dust, somewhere there was sun. Constant sun. Imagine that: warmth on your skin, all day every day. I go round to his place, big old house near where we used to go to school, and we listen to music. One song each, back-to-back, until he falls asleep and then I leave him there and head home. Hot shower before bed. Scalding heat and the feel of suds fizzing on my hands and fingers.

Patrick

I wanted to be better than this. When I was a kid, I wanted to have a bigger, bolder, more open life. And I've spent my life telling myself that I must, that to live any other way would be some sort of betrayal. Years congratulating myself for seeing the rules more clearly, seeing them for what they really are . . . not rules at all, habits made to look like choices. But when it comes down to it, when it came down to it, I don't actually think that. Not really. Not in my bones. Or even if I do think it, it doesn't matter, because I'm still not brave enough to live my life in the way that the knowledge demands of me. I'm the same as everyone else. Small, petty, jealous and fearful. And I fucking hate it.

It's all fine in theory. In theory I know that families can be suffocating, that they can channel our anger at the world into smaller and smaller, less threatening units, that they can make us tiny and grasping and protective and scared. But that's all it is, really, theory. Because when my own family happened, as if by magic, I was entirely sure that we were the exception to the rule. I no longer wanted freedom over possession. I wanted the things I loved to be mine. I'm not proud of feeling like that, but I accept it. I use the same old rules of thumb that everyone else does, marking out my life and my habits with them as if they might make me safer and less scared. As if they might protect me. When deep down I know full well that everyone has secrets and darknesses and an inner life that is probably really messed up, at least some of the time. And that you can't protect things for ever. That there is no such thing as a safe life. Part of me feels cowardly, feels like I gave up somewhere along the line, but most of me just feels that it is entirely normal to be white hot with anger at the thought of Shiv with someone else.

I know what Shiv would say, she would say I should feel how I want to feel, and that anger is fine, normal. That's always been the difference between us, she's a realist, willing to play in the mud and rot of life, to accept that things aren't always perfect and to forgive and muddle through. Whereas I'm here with my ideals, my theory, insulated and superior until the moment reality hits. In my head, the deal was that we would trade in all of our other possible lives, foreclose all of the other futures, let the world wall itself off, because we were trying to make something better. Trying to find some way of being that was kinder and less painful than the one we'd both known until then. And sometimes it felt like we were actually managing to, it really did. It felt like we had been given something delicate to take care of and to pass on. But where does that leave you, really? Walking a high wire, holding your breath and waiting for the fall? Shiv is right, always has been, it's too hard to live like that, unrealistic, you have to let the mess and the compromise in, drink it down, decide what matters and just keep walking. And anyway, where did all my ideals get me in the end? Spending my days delivering food that I couldn't afford to eat myself and letting myself get twisted up, get blinded to what really matters. Fucking pathetic.

I was only a kid when I first knew that I loved Shiv. From the moment I knew what it was to love someone, I loved her. We'd been friends for as long as I could remember, but something changed when we were about thirteen or fourteen. I started to think about her when music was playing, and to write her initials over and over and over again until the pen tore through the paper. I would find reasons to be near her . . . *yeah, I also need to go to the shop . . . I'll come with you . . . yeah, fuck PE, I'm not* doing it either . . . *I'll just fake a note and we can hang out*. Back then, I was learning quickly. On fire with the world. Reading about wars and markets and money and revolutionaries and scribbling slogans all over my schoolbooks and trainers. I did it because I was angry and because I meant it, but also because I thought it would impress Shiv. How could it not? Surely we all knew the world was shit and that it was only us who could change it? And then one day, we were walking to the bus stop and she just stopped me and said . . . *you know what? you were more fun before you got all peace peace save the whales.*

I didn't give a fuck about whales. It felt like she'd kicked me in the throat when she said that. Fucking whales. But the next day we kissed. And a few weeks later I told her I didn't care about whales and she laughed so much at my sad face that she said she was going to piss herself. And the whales stayed with us. For years, every time I would get too angry about something, Shiv would pull me in to her and whisper between kisses . . . *peace peace save the whales . . . peace peace save the whales*. And something would always fall away when she did that. We are working our way back towards each other. Or to be more accurate, I'm working my way back towards her. Trying to get over myself. And we'll get there.

A few nights ago I was out on a delivery to one of the other estates. I'd decided it was my last of the night. When I get there, the bloke is hanging off his balcony shouting that he will throw down his fob to let me in the block. I told him he had to come down. He told me he would throw down the fob. I told him he had to come down. Repeat. Until the cunt turned. Jeering at me, a look of total disgust on his face. Like I was nothing to him. Invisible in high-vis. I saw the spit, the phlegm catch the light as it looped from his mouth and towards me.

Landing about a metre away, thick and yellow and rancid. I just left his food on the pavement and rode off, but by the time I had got home I was shaking with anger. And with shame. I was ashamed because I was scared. Because I was scared that some supervisor who I would never meet would get an automated complaint about me and I wouldn't be able to work any more. Ashamed because I was scared of a world that made me work like this and was making more and more of us do it every single day, falling into it, falling beneath the line. Beneath the eyeline. I tell Shiv this and the more I speak, the more the tears come. She doesn't say *peace peace save the whales*. But she touches me in a way that makes me remember it. And that night we fucked as though we were trying to make another kid. Like we were both growing something. Making something.

Conor

Oli is speaking to me. Or at me. Always a bit of both with him. It's hard to lock in and register his words, I'm running on precisely zero hours' sleep and fighting through the heavy haze that is left when the vodka buzz has gone. The words keep coming. *Don't take it the wrong way . . . and anyway, I wasn't going to say anything . . . but I was talking to Rian last night, not about you really, you just came up . . . but it turns out we'd both seen you . . . walking about, late . . . night stalking like a paedo . . . just kidding, but seriously mate, it's not good to be doing that . . . come and hang out at Rian's place if you're bored . . . listen to records, his taste is shit and the fucker falls asleep by ten . . . but it's better than being on your own . . . that's no good . . . seriously . . . you should trust me on that, it's no good at all . . . I used to do it, remember? . . . I used to say I was sorting my head out . . . but I wasn't, not really . . . too much time on your own makes your head worse . . . cloudy . . . clouds up your nut . . .*

I can't seem to get through enough of the fog to answer him properly, to say the things I need to say to get him to stop talking for a bit. And I hate the idea of him talking about me with Rian. I know he's a mate, but I can't have him thinking I'm going to fuck this whole thing up, thinking he's got some loon in charge of things, can't have that. I can't fail at this. I can feel myself nodding, he'll wrap it up if I just keep nodding . . . *I'm not having a go, seriously . . . but think about it yeah? . . . next time you want to go out on one of your night-time nonce strolls, drop me a text, yeah?* Yeah.

I saw Sophie last night. For the first time in weeks. Something that had been fraying in me finally gave up and just snapped. You might as well swing for the things you love. People will tell you that there is some sort of dignity in letting things go, in acceptance, but fuck them. You fight for things until the fight is over, that's what I was always taught. The motorway was empty by the time I started out, almost midnight and already half cut. It stretched out like a thick vein carrying black blood, each city and each town an organ quietly pulsing with life. I thought of a picture I used to have on my bedroom wall, a lifetime ago. A motorway at night, with a shock of white light running down the middle, like a slash of paint or the crack of sun against darkness. Even as a kid I knew what the light meant. I knew it meant movement, that even though the picture was perfectly still, it was moving somehow. I remember asking my old man if it looked all blurry like that because the cars were moving so fast, but he explained that it was time-lapse photography that made it like that and that the cars were probably just moving at a normal speed. I didn't care. It looked like speed to me; it looked like leaving. I wondered if I had ever been in one of those pictures, a tiny piece of the blur, of the whiteness and of the light. And if I had, how old was I? Where was I driving when I was pinned there for ever, obliterated by movement?

I called her ten times. Twenty. No answer. Just about sober enough to know that knocking the door in the middle of the night wouldn't do much to help my cause. I just wanted to see Sean, just for a second, tell Sophie that I'm sorry, that I'm sick, that I can't get better without them. I sent a message. Re-sent it. Re-sent it again. Over and over. *Please come out or I'll have to knock the door . . . please . . . we just need to talk . . . ten minutes . . . please.* And then finally. A pattern of lights. I imagined it first as her phone, lighting up through the skin of her pillow. And then the bedroom light, the landing, the hallway and then finally the front door, cracking open and meeting the night air. Sophie walked towards me in oversized running trainers I recognised as being her dad's. A brand you haven't been able to buy in shops for years, but still in weirdly good nick. Fastidious. Mad what you end up focusing on, the stupid details you know will be there whenever you think back to that moment. Sophie was standing over me. *No I won't sit down . . . no I really won't sit down . . . no you can't come in . . . no not even for a minute . . . yes, you will wake him . . . you always wake him . . .* I stood up, reached out to touch her, to beg really. To beg for something. But she pushed me away. And then it was done. Before I could say anything else she was gone again, lights clicking off one by one and then back to the feeling of cold brick against the back of my legs. The cold brick against the back of my legs. Fixated. I ran my hands against the grooves in the cement, checking the lines and the lay. Imagined the hands of the person laying them, imagined them standing back every few minutes to check that they were flush. And I pushed down the urge to smash in the door, pull Sophie out, by her fucking hair if I had to, make her speak, make her let me feel the tiny warm body of my own fucking child pressed against my chest. But I didn't do that. I let the cold of the brick knife through to the back of my thighs for a few minutes longer and then I left.

    I left and it felt like an ending, like maybe there should have been loose ends and second chances and false restarts, but there weren't and there won't be. Escape velocity. How it takes almost all of the fuel to get a rocket out of the earth's atmosphere but then after that it will basically run on air. Leaving is like that too: takes all of your energy to do it but once you have broken through the membrane of the place that is holding you, it is all over. And maybe they were both better off there anyway, better off somewhere else. There is something dark here sometimes, and it can suck the life out of you. Maybe there is something dark in me too. I don't want to suck the life out of the people I love.

    In the distance, I can see Oli, three or four metres up, legs hanging off the scaffold, swinging free in the air. I can't hear exactly what he is saying, but I can tell he's telling stories to the lads in between bites of his sandwich. Feels like an odd thing to say considering how fucked up he used to be, but there's nothing dark in Oli. He's got his problems, but that lad is all light. I think of the man who used to be on site all of those years ago, reading his Bible on his break and never joining in. I wonder if he is still alive. He'd be old by now; I wonder if it did him any good, if any of his prayers amounted to anything. There's a momentum to endings, to falling apart. When something starts to crumble the rest is an inevitability. Build a brand-new house and then leave it alone for five years, make sure nobody lives there, that nobody touches it, and then open the front door and see what you find. You'll find rot and warp and things won't feel right in ways that you can't quite put your finger on. Maybe it's best to just go with the falling apart sometimes. Enough with the building and the Bibles. Maybe just go with it.

So I do just that. I go with it. They still ask every day . . . *pint? pub? . . . come on . . . just the one?* And this time I say yes. Oli looks pleased. He thinks I'm saying yes because of his rant this morning and not because my hands are still shaking from no sleep and drinking until the sun came up and I'm in desperate need of a straightener. The pub manages to seem somehow too bright and too dim all at once, and I can feel myself giving in as soon as I am in there. I can feel the hunger growing, the desire for blackout, wanting to end the night in total nothingness. And before I know it I am that twat . . . *one more . . . stay for one more . . . on me . . . I've got a tab . . . nah, you can all have tomorrow off . . . anyone got a line . . . or a bump at least . . . anyone up for afters somewhere else?* But by the end of the night I am on my own, one last drink and holding on to the bar to keep myself standing. I can feel the varnished wood of the bar underneath my fingers as I grip it for balance. The same thought circling . . . *I don't know why they do that to wood . . . wood is not supposed to be shiny . . . that is not how wood is supposed to be.*

Shiv

Patrick is back in our bed, thank god. It's taken a bit of time, but I can feel us coming back together. The flat is getting warmer day by day. For weeks, whenever we spoke the words seemed feeble and frail, like they were going to die in the air before they reached the other person. But recently, they've been getting stronger, managing to make it over the divide before they fall away. I would never say this to him, actually I'd be happy if we never talked about me and Rian again for as long as I fucking live, but there have been a few moments where I've even wondered if maybe this might have been good for us. Talking it all out, remembering how we were back then, those couple of years of not knowing if we would make it. It can be so easy to forget that we actually chose this. That there were other ways we could have been and lived, but that we chose this one and then we built it. These last few nights I've found myself reaching for Patrick in the night, feeling the cold outside air still clinging to his body as he tries to climb into bed without disturbing me. But I've wanted him to disturb me, to come to me. I want to feel his long, thin legs pushing mine apart. It's turned greedy and urgent. I am always ready for him. I don't tell him to come inside me. He just looks into my eyes and I answer him by wrapping my legs around his back and pulling him deeper.

The phone rings out to start with, stopping before I'm fully awake. But the second time it rings, it manages to find its way deeper into my dreams, first as a distant car alarm and then as a siren screeching past me as I'm about to cross the road, pulling me closer to consciousness each time. The third time it rings, it wakes me. It must be my phone, Patrick always leaves his charging downstairs. I grope for it in the darkness, my hand finding it by the side of the bed and immediately flicking the ringer to silent. The screen is flashing Oli's name. Half asleep, my brain thinks he's probably just fucked, blissed out and incoherent and wanting someone to babble to. But then I remember it's been ages since Oli has been like that, at least in front of people, and anyway, why is he even phoning me, he never phones me. I pick up. There's a forced politeness in his voice. Too fast. *Shiv I'm so sorry to wake you, really sorry . . . I tried Patrick but his phone is just ringing out . . . is he there? . . . so sorry again to wake you.* I ask if it can wait, looking over at Patrick's sleeping body and not wanting to wake him, not wanting to pull him out of sleep. I ask if Oli can leave a message. Maybe I could write it across Patrick's beautiful sleeping eyelids with a feather. It can't wait apparently. I shake Patrick gently by the shoulder until he wakes.

I can hear most of it. Oli's voice is loud against the wind, cutting through the silence of our bedroom . . . *have you heard from him . . . I know I know but seriously mate you didn't see him . . . I'm worried about him . . . something doesn't seem right . . . I know I know . . . intuition . . . something really off at the pub . . . seriously off.* I watch Patrick slowly pull his body up against the headboard, pressing his knuckles into his eyes and trying to wake himself up properly. The light of the phone is illuminating the side of his face and I notice how deep some of the cracks around his mouth are. Patrick is using the voice he uses when he is trying to calm people down . . . *I get that mate, I do . . . but we should wait . . . it's only been a few hours . . . seriously . . . go home and get some rest and if he doesn't turn up at the site tomorrow just ring me straight away . . . there is nothing to be done tonight mate, it's probably nothing . . . go to sleep . . . promise me.*

The thing is, Patrick is wrong. I know Conor has something stupid in him, always has done. Patrick thinks too much of his friends sometimes, imagines they are the same as they were when they were kids ready to take on the world. Sometimes he misses the wear and tear they've taken, how ground down they have got. And he doesn't know how bad Sophie got before she left, those days when she seemed to be unravelling. There was something seriously dark eating at her, hard to place, but something like panic. Maybe even fear. There were times when she seemed scared of Conor. It's not easy for me to imagine he might have done something stupid, crossed a line, hit her, but it's not impossible for me to imagine either. I just get the sense that she's gone. For good. None of that headspace or trial separation bullshit, I reckon she is fully gone. From the few messages she's sent me since, she already seems distant and closed off. If I were placing a bet, I reckon Conor will never see that kid again. And I'd bet that Conor knows it too.

And now my mind is racing through memories of Conor. The intensity of him sometimes, the way he always seemed ever so slightly removed from Patrick and Rian and Oli. Always the quickest to throw a punch when we were kids, the most willing to do something daft, an image of him writhing on the floor, leg broken from jumping off a balcony for a dare. And later, the nights out with him. Especially when I was pregnant the first time, still wanting to go out but staying sober while they all got fucked up. Those were the times I really noticed. Conor would get fucked in a different way; even when Oli was at his worst, there was still something about the way Conor got fucked up that made you feel the most uneasy. Something utterly relentless. As everyone else started to unknot and untangle, he seemed to get more tightly wound as the night went on, jaw swinging, and then blacking out, all of a sudden and all at once, while the rest of them faded much more gradually out of focus. Everyone else was too messed up to notice. But I noticed. It set me on edge then and, remembering it now, it is setting me on edge all over again.

The more I picture it, the more the panic starts to work its way up my spine. Patrick has got this wrong. I used to hate the idea of intuition; round here everyone's mom or nan reads the tea leaves or the cards, dangling bits of string over your belly when you're pregnant. But I feel something like that now, a bad feeling that can't find its way into words. I find my hands reaching for Patrick again . . . *Patrick, something doesn't feel right . . . I can't sleep . . . Oli wouldn't ring for no reason . . . you should ring him back.* He can see that I'm serious and puts his hand out for my phone. Redials the number . . . *O.K. mate, O.K., give me ten minutes or so and I'll be there . . . just stay where you are . . . yeah, whatever, call Rian if you like, I don't give a fuck . . . just stay where you are and I'll be there as soon as I can.*

I'm glad Rian will be there too, but I can see that Patrick isn't. I watch him pull his trousers over his hips . . . *it will be fine, I really love you . . . ring me when you hear anything, O.K.? . . . no, no, don't worry about waking me up.* I know I won't go back to sleep at this point. It's only a few hours before the sun will be up and flooding through the room, catching the windows of the flats opposite. I won't go back to sleep at this point. I listen to Patrick wrangle his bike. Familiar sounds. The click of the front door and then the sound of the key turning gently in the lock. The silence as he heads down in the lift, and then finally the distant hiss of wheels, his bike against the wet pavement.

Patrick

I wasn't worried at first, just pissed off that Oli had woken us up. A few seconds of that slightly unreal feeling, in the half space between sleep and consciousness, and then a sudden wave of irritation. I thought maybe Oli had just taken things a bit too far in the pub, or maybe even lapsed a bit into something worse. But it wasn't that. He sounded frantic and insistent. I know Conor has been having a rough time recently, I mean, fuck, I can barely imagine what it must be like to think you're losing your family. But honestly, like I say, I wasn't worried at first. I still thought Oli was overreacting. Conor is a grown man. Grown men are allowed to disappear. It was only when Shiv woke me again and I saw the panic in her, that's when I changed my mind. Dragged myself up and out, automatic movements in the darkness.

The first few minutes of riding are always grim. I'm cursing the rain, the wind blowing sheets of it against cheeks already stinging from the cold. But it's the same every time, once I've built up some speed, I start to feel the air sharpening me, prodding at my lungs and changing my breathing. Maybe Oli is right to be worried. Maybe I've taken my eye off the ball and Conor is more fucked up and broken than I realised. Maybe while I've been wallowing in my feelings about something from years ago, someone I love has been falling to pieces without me noticing. An image of Conor rises up and I can't shake it. I push the pedals down harder to try to drive it out of my head, but it won't leave. What if we turn up to the site and find him there? What if his body has been there for hours while we were all sleeping, swinging from some scaffold, getting soaked through with rain? I can see the rope cutting into his neck, redder and deeper by the minute. Surely not. There were always stories of cords arounds necks when we were kids, someone always knew someone who knew someone who had done it. But surely not Conor. Not even at the site, which to me already stinks of death. Parasitic. Sucking up the skyline, box after identical box, expensive shelter for cheap lives. Fuck Rian and fuck his fucking buildings while you are at it. There are days I ride past that place and want to burn it to the ground. Pull it off like a leech and let the blood run.

I turn the corner and I can see the site looming upwards, bigger every day, drawing everything towards it. Something like that shifts the centre of gravity, the newest thing becomes the centre, realigning the streets and the buildings around it. Something can be on the edge of a place, but if it's new enough and big enough, it becomes the fixed point of reference, the new heart, metallic and grafted on. The bigger it gets the harder it is to picture what was there before, the low roof of the Meadows, the old haunted faces at the window that used to scare the shit out of us. Was there something there before that, or just empty land, I wonder. Is there anyone left around here who would remember?

As I get closer I can see that Oli is already there with Rian. Something like anger rises in me but then quickly softens into something more like relief. They wouldn't both be standing there like that if they had found Conor swinging from some fucking scaffolding, surely. Thank god. They must have checked. Oli knows the site like the back of his hand by now, must do, even in the dark. How big is this place, exactly? Not so big you would miss a human body. Oli will know. I get off my bike and lean it against what I think is a wall. But the bricks haven't been cemented yet and the weight of the bike knocks a few of them tumbling . . . *fuck . . . he's not here then? . . . you've checked . . . everywhere . . . and what about the less obvious places? . . .* Oli says he has, but that it was hard with only a torch, that it will be easier when the sun starts to come up . . . *I do think he's been here though, mate . . . there's a chance at least . . . the gate to the place where we keep all the equipment was unlocked . . . someone could have just forgotten to lock it . . . I've forgotten loads of times . . . but still . . .*

There's no point us all standing here in the rain talking about keys and gates, so I suggest that we split up and look for him. Rian nods in agreement. We haven't spoken any words out loud to each other in months, and neither of us seems to know how to break the silence. Oli will trace the route back from the pub to the site and keep trying to get hold of Sophie as well, see if he might have made some drunken dash to try to see her. Oli says that apparently Conor was slurring something about that in the pub last night, something about her not letting him in, making him sit on some little wall, something about her dad's trainers. Sounds like he was totally out of it. I'll take the park and the rec and the lake; it will be easier for me to cover on my bike, especially when the ground is so wet. Rian can take the house . . . *If he doesn't answer the door and you can't see anything, just smash one of the windows . . . we can get it sorted in the morning if we have to . . . it's not like we don't know enough fucking builders.*

The park opens up off the right-hand side of the main road. I must pass it twenty times a day. You can't see it from the bottom of the hill, but after a certain point in the climb it springs into view, a big, open, bare space, the first few metres catching the spill-over from the streetlights, but dark as you like beyond that. As I turn in, I clock the community noticeboard, upright and blank near the entrance. The noticeboard has an events section that is empty, an information section that is also empty and a community section that has a faded leaflet offering house clearance and gardening services. It would be less depressing, by some distance, if they just took the noticeboard down.

A hundred metres or so into the park and I hit what we used to call the bomb mound. It is a sort of artificial hill that we used to roll down as kids and then BMX down as teenagers. Rumours and whispers meant that we were all sure the mound was covering an unexploded bomb from the Second World War. It was a bit depressing when the internet finally arrived and the local history page described it not as an unexploded bomb but as an old air raid shelter. I push my bike over the top of the mound, not wanting to risk the steep incline in the rain. I feel the crosses of rusted metal that still peek through the grass. Twenty times a day I pass this place and I hardly ever turn in. And here I am in the dark and the wet looking for Conor, wondering whether to start shouting his name, getting totally flooded with memory. School trips we took here, despite the fact our school was no more than ten minutes' walk away. Conor putting insects into plastic tubs and ticking them off on his worksheet, threatening to shake the spiders and the centipedes onto someone's head. Conor during that weird canoeing thing on the lake when there weren't nearly enough canoes for everyone to have a go. Fishing someone's braces out of the water with the oar and everyone cheering, how hot it was under those thick life jackets, the machinic dance of gnats around our sticky foreheads. The same lake I fell into, years later. Conor laughing as loud as anyone.

How many first kisses in this park, how many first fucks? Sheets of rain now, streetlights too distant to be useful, no movement ahead of me, the park stretching out into the distance. If I turn back and look towards the road, I can see the outline of some of the taller flats, the odd light left on while people sleep, or people waking early to work through the early hours. But straight ahead of me, there is nothing. The sound of the bike wheels pressing into the mud. Wet enough to feel like something other than solid ground.

Rian

I've been falling asleep early recently. Sometimes I even sleep for a few hours in the middle of the day. I wondered if I might be sick, but I think it's just the coming back that has done it. I'm sinking back into my life again, feeling the texture of it between my toes. Breathing a bit more slowly, catching up on years of late nights and fitful, frantic mornings.

So at first I thought it might be early when my phone woke me, maybe Oli was bored and wanted to come round for a few hours. I only caught the time in the corner of the phone screen right as I was about to answer, too late to properly register it. Oli is good these days, most of the time at least. But it's hard to shake a lifetime of feeling worried and protective over someone, so at first I assumed something bad had happened to him . . . *mate . . . calm down, take a breath . . . just tell me what's wrong.* But Oli is fine, it's Conor that he's worried about . . . *seriously mate, I know you think I'm overreacting, but you didn't see him in the pub . . . totally out of it, spiralling . . . all sorts of shit, think he went to see Sophie and it spun him . . . hard to get any sense . . . I shouldn't have left him there, but it was fucking hard to watch . . . the other lads must have thought the same because apparently he refused to leave when they all finally fucked off home.* As Oli is talking I remember seeing Conor a few weeks back, walking about in the middle of the night. Oli had seen him do it too. We'd done nothing about it. Just watched him. I hang up on Oli and tell him I'll try Conor's phone. He always picks up when I call him, which embarrasses me a bit, but it might be useful at this precise moment. No answer. No answer again.

I call Oli back and tell him to come to my house and we can figure out what to do from there. But he's already heading to the site. Patrick is meeting us there too, apparently. My chest tightens a bit at the thought of seeing him, even though I want to, and even though it would have been ridiculous of Oli not to call him. It's idiotic for us to carry on like this, but I'm still so ashamed of my behaviour that night, of all the fucking stupid things I said. It still runs through me whenever I think of it, setting my jaw on edge, tight with self-loathing.

I can walk to the site from my house. It takes some time, but I still haven't managed to get rid of my stupid car, and I feel a bit of a cunt whenever I drive it, so I walk. But by the time I'm halfway there, I regret it. The rain is heavy and at least the car would have given us somewhere warm to sit and talk. As long as we did it only two at a time. I push on until I can see the outline of the site in the distance. It looks intense at night; when buildings aren't finished your eyes don't automatically recognise the shapes of them, imperfect and incomplete. Fuck me though, it's coming on. Slow start, but Conor is doing a good job of things by the looks of it. And I say by the looks of it, because if I'm totally honest, I don't care that much. I wanted to help Conor, and I wanted Conor to be able to help Oli, to keep him busy. And I needed a plausible reason to stay anchored to this place, when I was feeling it slip away, coming back to visit less and less. But beyond that, it didn't bother me, it wasn't big money, and I'd doubted some of Conor's promises from the beginning. If it comes out even, that'll be fine by me. More recently it's given me an excuse when people ask why I've moved back here. A building project makes more sense to people than saying . . . *I thought I got my heart broken by this rich woman who smelled amazing but turned out to be quite cruel . . . but actually I think I was just empty and regretful and lonely and desperate to see things I knew and loved every morning and also the noise and the river had started to thud through me like a sickness and I was nauseous almost all of the time and so so tired oh and also did I mention I was lonely* . . .

Patrick arrives a few minutes after me. He proceeds to knock down a wall with his bike and then immediately launches into that tone he uses when he has decided to be an irritating officious cunt. It's the same tone he used back in the days when you had to book taxis hours in advance to get home after a night out . . . *no, not one more round . . . the car will be here in ten minutes and also you still owe me your seven-quid share* . . . Despite this, I am glad he is there, and I want to tell him that. But I can't. Or I don't. The words keep catching on my tongue and then I swallow them back down. He seems as awkward as me, directing all of his words at Oli instead. I've known him long enough to know he has had some of the same thoughts as me over the last hour or so. Thoughts of Conor's body folded up next to a cement mixer or swinging from a rafter or a beam. I can see the fear of it in his eyes. I want to stay calm, but I think we're infecting one another with panic. Oli is the most level-headed. Even in the midst of all this, that still seems noteworthy. He tells us Conor isn't on the site, but he might have been here. When he says this, some of the worst images start to fall away and dissolve.

I feel guilty having to check that Conor still lives at the same address. He does. And then I feel guilty again for having to ask for the postcode so I can put it into my phone. I should know this stuff. It is so quiet on the walk over. Not so long ago, I lived in a place that would have still been humming with taxis and parties and dealers and twenty-four-hour newsagents selling samosas and scratch cards. But here there is no sound other than the rain dotting against leaves and windshields. Are all of these people asleep? How many of them are dreaming and what are they dreaming about? I imagine each house I pass, flicking between bedrooms like a bored teenager flicking between cable channels. Dreams of intense, surreal colours, mundane dreams of commuting and anxiety, dreams of flesh and of tongues. I think of Conor somewhere, dreaming his own dreams, a dream of dead leaves and warm wind, a dream of remnants and rubble. No answer at his door. I knock the window for good measure, nothing. Intensely aware of how quiet everything is, I take off my coat and wrap it around my fist before I smash the kitchen window. It works: no blood and no sound. I reach in to open the window from the inside and then jump up to edge myself through. Fuck me, it's harder than it should be. I'm getting fat, or old. Or both. It's both.

The state of it. It can't have been that long since Sophie left, but Conor has managed to turn this place upside down. It's halfway between the IKEA catalogue and a particularly grim crack den. There are open pizza boxes on the floor, most with only a slice or two eaten from them. A puddle of lager pooling on the kitchen surface, ants gathering in its sweetness. And glass. Glass fucking everywhere. Some from the smashed window, but more from the smashed bottles, scattered and jagged like half-formed stars. Waiting for a universe to begin. As I turn the corner into the hallway, I half expect to find him crumpled at the bottom of the stairs and breathe a sigh of relief when there is nothing there. Heading up the stairs, I make a ritual of calling his name every second step, like some sort of rosary. No answer. In the bedroom, it is as though I have gone back in time to whenever Sophie and Sean were still here. The bed is perfectly made, blankets on the cot turned down at the edges, untouched. Where has he been sleeping? I open the wardrobe because I've seen people do it in films. All of his clothes seem to be there. So he hasn't left, or if he has, he's left in a hurry. I reach out and run my hand along the rows of clothes, thin T-shirts in various colours, hoodies with chewed drawstrings, a single suit gone shiny with age, a pair of work boots that look as though they are made of clay. The smell of washing powder and soap.

Conor

... I don't know why they do that to wood ... wood is not supposed to be shiny ... that is not how wood is supposed to be.

Everyone is gone. They were here just a second ago; did they all leave when I was in the toilet? How long was I in the fucking toilet? The old lad who runs the place has his hand on my shoulder, guiding me out the door and telling me to go home and sleep it off. This isn't the type of thing you can sleep off, but I'm yeah yeah-ing him just to get him out of my face.

The world is spinning so I slump down against the pebbledash wall of the building. Just for a second, just to get my bearings. I'm looking out at the estate in front of me, wet ground starting to soak through the back of my jeans. And I hate it, I hate this place. It has sucked me in like a sinkhole and the sludge has slowly turned me putrid. Maybe Sophie was right to leave, bring Sean up somewhere else, somewhere less weighed down by layer upon layer of stupid stories, passed around and retold. I don't want my son hearing the same shit I've been hearing for thirty years, some story about the old days where the hero changes depending on who is telling it and who is around to contradict them. Gold rings getting tighter around fat, red fingers, making you want to saw through the band and give the person a bit of relief. Tattoos drained of colour, fading first to green and then to the pale blue of smudged biro. Enough. I was stupid to think I could make something new here. We're just making the same old mistakes. Even if I manage to finish them, the new flats would go to shit within a decade, cheap materials, unsafe and untested, filling the sky for a while and then taking their turn to crumble.

I managed to get a gram from one of the younger lads before he left . . . *yes, I'm fucking sure . . . just hand it over* . . . Pushing twenty-pound notes into his hand and then touching the plastic in my pocket every five minutes to check that it is still there. I can't rack it into lines in this rain so I'm digging my key into the powder and pushing it into my nose. Bump after bump until I can feel the chemical swirl in my chest. It feels as if my heart is growing, getting bigger and bigger until it is pushing against the inside of my ribs, trying to escape for air. Another bump and I could open my throat and suck in this entire night, then breathe deeper and suck in the entire estate. Everything covered in darkness. Holding it in my stomach until I spit it back out again, drenched in the light of morning. I swear we used to do this type of thing in bars and clubs, not on the ground in pub car parks, in the rain. Sophie even did a line off my cock once. I close my eyes and picture her laughing face looking up at me. I dig my key into the corner of the packet again, fishing out powder from the edges. I want every grain, as though I am hungry, starving. As though I haven't eaten in days.

Looking at the key reminds me of something. As I lick the remnants from the ridge that runs down its centre, I remember I have another bottle in the locked Portakabin at the site. Best to always have one there in case you need to steady your hands in the morning. The effort of pulling myself off the ground, and then the steady stagger, being drawn towards what I need, step by step. I want that familiar mineral burn in my throat, the heat of it, I can almost taste the blackout already, the freezing floor against my face and the prospect of tomorrow's sun stabbing me awake.

This is taking forever. How many wrong turns can you take in a place you've known your whole life? The silence is throwing me off, disorientating me. When did everyone I know start sleeping so much? All anyone seems to do is sleep; where are the insomniacs when you need them? Minutes of walking without even seeing a light on. Eventually I fall against the gate, press my key into the lock, that last half-bump fizzing between my eye sockets and my cheekbones.

People think I love the site, because I'm always here. But I don't. I'm here all the time because I don't know what to do with myself. And because things are getting so bad that I've started to feel like if I am here all of the time, the place will forgive me. It's an act of service and submission; I'm begging the place not to kill me, hoping it responds to loyalty and prayer. People let me down in the early months, half promises, prices raised at the last minute. I was naive. I've cut every corner since, trying to claw things back, but even if everything goes perfectly from this moment on, I'll be left with fuck all to show for it. The last thing I had to offer, slipping away a bit more with every invoice. So I walk around here at night, trying to reason with the place like it's some sort of angry god. Asking it to save me in the way it was always supposed to. Asking it to take away the image I see every time I close my eyes. Sophie on the kitchen floor, making herself small in front of me.

I look in my backpack and the bottle is almost full, thank fuck. I drink it like water, feeling the edges of the world begin to fall away. I am all fuzz, ears ringing and then sharpening into a whine. The cabin is in and out of focus. I can see it better if I close one eye. Things that people have made to help people make other things. Wrenches and hammers, post-drivers and flat mallets, new bricks wrapped in cellophane. And then I can see my hands as they tear through the plastic. As they lift each brick, stacking them one on top of the other until my backpack is full and heavy. I'm good at carrying bricks. Back to where I started. Just left school and feeling the weight of burnt clay on my back.

The walk is a struggle, shoulders starting to burn, but I

know that if I stop I won't start again. Obvious what needs to be done. Clearest I have been in years. All that noise and then suddenly the sound just snaps back in.

The grass is soaking underfoot, wet through, rain clinging against my eyelashes. There is just enough light from the moon to catch the edges of the beer cans that are scattered around the lake, lighting them up like a constellation. The lip of the water. I am perched on the rim of the world, and I know exactly what I am supposed to do. The weight of the bricks, the sound of them gritting together as I move. The first shock of the cold water and then the feeling of it running into my skull and then finally into my lungs. Ice turning to burning heat and then slowly fading again. Warm now. The feel of her skin on my skin. Warm now. The shine of scaffolding caught by the sun. Warm now. My hand resting on the back of our old television. Warm now.

Four

Patrick

It feels as though everyone I know is here. And in some strange way, maybe even more than that, almost like everyone I have ever *seen* is here. I get the sense that every face I have ever passed in the street is here. That every face that has ever opened the door to me, careful not to meet my eyes when I hand over their food, is here. Every face that has ever bled into my dreams . . . they are all here. Flattened into composites and distributed across the fifty or so people who are milling around the church hall, waiting for something to begin. Everyone I have ever seen is here. Except Sophie. Who definitely isn't here. In any sense. Which is something everybody has noticed but that nobody is mentioning. I know why she isn't here, and on balance, I'm glad. The things Shiv has told me about what went on between her and Conor make my skin crawl, make me ball up my fist in my pocket. It splinters things, makes me wonder if I could have stopped it years ago, if we all might have been able to bleed the bile out of him somehow, rather than let it fester the way it did, damaging all the people he loved. Maybe that's no use to anybody now though, too late for him and too late for Sophie and Sean, no point dragging a body from the water just to put it on trial, and no point making someone a devil when they are already a ghost. At least not today.

I don't think Conor was religious. If he was, he never talked about it. Or not properly at least, not directly. When we were kids we would talk about all of the big questions . . . *how did we get here and is there life after death and are there aliens and is there such a thing as love?* But only in that way that kids do before they start to get embarrassed about being interested in things. And then again a bit later, when we were all taking a lot of drugs but were too poor to go to clubs and distract ourselves with dancing. At that point the questions came again, *is this all there is do you think? . . . are you and I really just the same person? . . . how sure are you that you are actually alive?* All of those were religious questions too, but not in a way that means his funeral should be in a church with a priest mumbling over his body.

But that's just how it's done here. Whether it's a reflex or not is hard to tell, but whenever something bad happens, the prayers just start tripping off people's tongues, the hands start reaching for the rosary beads. I can see some of them doing it now, under their breath, muttering things that they were taught a thousand Sundays ago. People's funeral clothes have got too big or too small since the last time they were needed. Top buttons that won't quite fasten, jackets billowing around the stomach, and the odd few with no jackets at all, making do with dark winter coats over their shirts and ties until it seems O.K. to take them off.

The women have done better than the men. A middle ground of black and charcoal dresses with only a few diverging at the extremes, a couple of older women in the type of elaborate veils that I thought only existed in insurance adverts and a couple of younger cousins whose dresses are so tight and so short that it is obvious they are treating the funeral as pre-drinks. Everyone is fussing with something, dancing around one another while they organise the food, or reaching into their inside pockets to take a nip from a hip flask when they think nobody is looking. Rituals layered on top of rituals. The patterns that tell you what to do in situations when there is really nothing to be done. When people die, these rituals start to make total sense. There's nothing to be done, so we silently decide to move together, swoop and leap in patterns like a murmur of black starlings.

I know when people are drunk enough they will start to ask me. I found Conor that night, so I'm the closest thing they have to an answer. I'll tell them that yes it was a shock, that yes I was on my own but people came quickly, that yes he had been going through such a rough time. I won't tell them that the only reason I even saw him was because the backpack had slipped off his shoulders and let his body rise to the surface. And I won't tell them that his face was already blue and bloated but that there was something calm about his eyes. And I won't tell them that he looked worse on the bank among the cans and the rubbish than he did floating in the dirty water, or how the noise of the ambulance finally broke through the quiet of the night or how its flashing light cut across the grass and illuminated his face for a few seconds. I won't tell them that as soon as I saw him, I understood. And that they would have understood too if they had been the ones to find him.

Shiv is sitting with Oli, who is entertaining Molly and Freya with some sort of basic magic trick. She is trying to calm and shush them every time they shriek with gleeful disbelief and try to snatch the cards to make sense of the mystery. I'm so glad she is here. Just like I was glad she was there this morning when I was behind her, helping her to zip up her dress, and I collapsed into ugly, heavy sobs, burying my head in the back of her hair. Rian comes over and asks if I am O.K. and then immediately says that is a stupid question. Which it is. But I still ask him the same question in return. There is still something hanging between us, maybe there always will be. Something that means I can't make the words come out quite right without feeling embarrassed and then feeling angry that I feel embarrassed. But I am glad he is here too. I am glad everyone is here.

At the service, there is church music. Hymns that nobody really knows, forcing us to mouth the words and catch the end syllables. They just about get carried along by the mandatory handful of trilling enthusiasts unleashing their shaky soprano and a few old lads who are already pissed enough to boom along without a care in the world. I look down the line at Oli and Shiv. The bad singing has raised a smile; Oli looks like he might be about to start laughing at any second. I look away so that he doesn't infect me.

The eulogies are painful, in both senses of the word. Relatives who fall apart with emotion before they have even started and then the priest droning on about Conor in a way that bears so little relationship to what he was actually like that I can feel Oli laughing on my shoulder again . . . *Conor was a mild man, he cared about his community* . . . That's enough for Oli, who is not quite whispering . . . *Mild? . . . mild? . . . I have seen the man drink a shot of his own piss . . . more than once!* This sends Shiv over the edge and she audibly snorts. I hold on to her arm, which is shaking with the effort of keeping the laughter in.

After the eulogies, there are two readings. Me and one other. They asked me to read a poem. I've no idea why. I think someone got the idea that because I like books, I must also like poems. I do not. And I'm not sure anyone else here does either. I suppose it is just another ritual. Death happens or marriage happens and you reach for the ritual of elevated speech, rest it on your tongue for a few seconds like a communion wafer. I am worried that I have chosen something too literal, that it might offend people or feel too close to the bone. But I must have looked through a hundred or more, and this was the only one that felt right. I've practised it twice at home, but by the time I get to the end, my voice has failed and cracked . . . *shut up the stars and bury the ash in the earth . . . and, in the rising of the light, wake with those who awoke . . . or go on in the dream, reaching the other shore . . . of the sea that has no other shore.*

Rian

This room is making me dizzy. I keep working my finger between my collar and neck as if it might have the effect of magically loosening it. I'm too fat for this suit, which in turn is too heavy for this weather. Thick black merino wool with a lining that is so flamboyant I keep having to make sure you can't see it when I sit down. The last time I wore this was at the funeral of Emma's grandfather. I remember when she first told me he was ill and probably going to die soon. I was surprised, because she'd never mentioned him to me before, and also because I couldn't believe that she had a grandparent who was still alive. Rich people live a really long time.

Scanning the room I keep thinking that I am seeing people that I know. And maybe I do know them. But I can't place them and their names have slipped from my memory. I try to avoid talking to them in case it gets awkward. But people have other ideas. I've been back a little while now, but people are still treating me like a novelty. The older lads especially, one after another, coming up to me and patting the top of my arms with their heavy hands. It's drawing people's attention to me, and I hate it . . . *I hear you sorted the food . . . that's good of you son . . . and the drink too . . . you knew the boy well . . . horrible.* I seriously consider hiding in my car and getting Oli to text me when the service is starting.

We used to have school discos in this hall. Boys on one side and girls on the other, until the last half an hour when people got brave enough to shuffle around to the slow songs, ecstatic and awkward and perfect. Out of their uniform and dressed up like highlighter pens, every single girl seemed unbearably beautiful. The outline of their simple underwear that I'd imagine later as lace, shine on their forehead from two hours of dancing, the crust of concealer struggling to cover an acne outbreak, and the constant smell of vanilla body spray. I actually stole some of that vanilla body spray from a chemist once. I'd spray some into the lid and then sniff it while I touched myself, running through images of the girls in my class like I was taking an attendance register. Huffing cheap deodorant while I wanked. This is where my mind goes, minutes before we're about to bury one of my best friends in the dirt.

It goes there, and it goes somewhere else as well. A different funeral. To the day we buried Patrick's mom, all those years ago, and that sick, burning jealousy I felt watching him and Shiv comfort one another. I shouldn't have run away with that still sitting in my stomach. Sometimes I wonder if that was the moment that everything went bad. Maybe I knocked something loose that is still unravelling now.

Since the night Conor died, every hour has seemed like a week, nerves exposed, an open wound. Every time I close my eyes and try to sleep, I can hear Patrick's voice on the phone, and the sound of my feet slapping heavily against the pavement as I started running towards the park. I was in Conor's bedroom when Patrick called, and I had instinctively reached out and grabbed the coat that was hanging in his cupboard. As if that is what a person who has drowned themselves in a lake needs . . . a fucking coat. I was cradling the thing over my arm like an idiot, panting and breathless up the hill, dreading what I would see when I got there. The light of the ambulance and the police cars. Me, last to arrive, trundling and trailing and carrying this fucking coat.

I'm jolted back there every time my phone rings. And my phone rings a lot. People want to know what is happening with the site, whether they should bother going to work or not. I couldn't care less. If I had my way I would tear the entire thing down. Or blow it up, have everyone along to watch the way we used to do. Maybe we could even put a picture of the explosion up in the cafe next to the old one. It might feel good to blow something up that was only half finished, rather than something that had already started to fall apart. An Etch A Sketch. The drawing has taken a wrong turn, so let's rub it out and start again. Starting something is not a good enough reason to finish something. A sunk cost is still a cost. But I should talk to Oli about it before I make any final decisions. I know the place matters to him; maybe it mattered to Conor too. Or maybe he hated the place. Maybe it fucking killed him. I have no idea. I really wish I had spoken to him more.

Finally, the ceremony. All of us—me, Oli, Patrick, Shiv and the girls—take a row near the back. Molly and Freya are standing next to me, the closest I've been to them in months. Both of them are above waist height these days. I look directly down at the top of their heads, hair held in place with thin black hairbands, and I can feel the tears start to burn the back of my eyeballs. They are both starting to look so much like Patrick. I can picture him perfectly at their age, right down to which action figure he would have been obsessed with, dragging it around with him for the whole year. It's harder to see Shiv in them, but I wonder if that's because I don't really have a memory of her at their age. She is frozen for me at a different point. I can picture her as she is now, one of the best people I know, and I can picture her that night all those years ago, fixed in time. Everything in between is missing.

We'd taken a row near the back in case one of the girls got too upset and Patrick or Shiv had to bundle them out. But when it comes to it, we're the ones who threaten to cause a scene. There are eulogies. Some are incredibly sad, but a couple are so off base that Oli, in his eternal wisdom, decides to start whispering a running counter-commentary. Shiv is the closest to cracking, and I am thankful that she just about keeps it together. If she had started, we would have all been laughing in seconds, collapsing like dominoes, kids in detention all over again.

Patrick is last to read. Every single person can see the pain in him, wrenching him, his knuckles turning white as he grips the lectern. When his voice starts to go, the tears that were earlier burning the back of my eyes start to run freely, settling in the patches on my face where I haven't shaved properly. I notice Shiv nodding at him, barely visible, urging him on. When he has finished and starts shuffling past me to get back to his seat, I desperately want to hold him. But I settle for one of those heavy, cowardly pats on the upper arm that I have been getting off the old lads all day . . . *well done mate . . . seriously . . .*

Shiv

I don't trust people who are good at funerals. Nobody likes funerals, obviously. Or nobody admits to liking them, at least. But some people are still good at them. Useful, organised, a gift for saying the right thing at the right time to the right person. I am none of the above. I hate funerals with a passion, and I am also totally shit at them. I hate to be around death, I hate to be reminded that someone I love is gone, and that one day everyone else I love will be gone too. Life and soul of the fucking party, me.

Already I can feel people starting to get under my skin. People are jockeying, quietly lobbying for the status of their own memories and their own pain. Who feels the most pain, who knew him best. It's like having someone else's hand pick at one of your scabs. They can't just let it be. Can't let you hold on to your own fractured picture. They want you to join them in pinning the person down like a dried flower, agreeing on the handful of anecdotes and stories that are permissible and repeatable. I don't want to be won over to some other person's version of events, have my images of Conor diluted and infected by theirs. Fuck that. They can leave my memories exactly where they are. I mean, I loved Conor, really loved him. But he was also a bit of a fuck-up, with a cruel laugh and reliably terrible shoes. He was big on ideas and short on execution, terrible on the drink, and when I think of what he did to Sophie towards the end, I run cold. But Conor was also incredibly kind, and in his own way, incredibly brave. And that's what you carry in the end, isn't it? The whole mess of a person, all the broken bits of them, even the bits that cut your hands, the bits you'd rather throw away. Nobody will say this about Conor, but if anyone was going to do this, to end things, it was always going to be him. And I mean, for fuck's sake, how can anyone really pretend to be shocked when we have all lived enough of this life to know full well the ways this shit just grinds you down? There are moments when I wonder if I could have done more for him, especially recently, let him know that we aren't defined by our very worst moments, that if you can change what you do, over and over, for a long enough time, it is almost as good as changing what you are. Other times it all just makes sense, the freedom that comes with saying enough is enough, no more of this.

All funerals are bad. But this one is shaping up to be bad in its own special way. The older lads have slicked their yellow-grey hair back with old school Brylcreem, running their hands through it and then leaving grease patches on the women's dresses when they hug. Breath and lips already rank with hip-flask booze. Rian has paid for everything today, sorting it all out on the quiet. Or so he thinks. Because it's not quiet. Money is never quiet to people who don't have it. They notice when it makes even the smallest sound. There is too much food, and it isn't covered in cling film, but in purpose-made catering trays with plastic lids. And the food itself is small, and it has allergy labels, and some of it is balanced on the end of thick spoons so you can eat it in one go while you are holding a drink. Speaking of which, there is also a free bar, which is confusing people so much that they keep insisting on paying and getting into arguments with the bar staff.

And I know this will happen. There will be a moment when someone gets drunk enough to start saying something stupid about what happened to Conor, about the sin of taking your own life and what God does and doesn't forgive. I can feel myself eyeing the room, wondering which one it will be. One of the old girls wearing a veil seems a likely bet. There is one in particular who looks like she is almost bursting to babble about angels and demons, magic and resurrection, the ways Satan can work through you if you don't stay on your guard. I can feel a hatred for her bubbling up in me and it reminds me that not only do I hate funerals, and not only am I bad at them, but that they also make me a bit mad. All I really want is to sit with Patrick, Oli and the girls, maybe Rian too if those two can stop being weird with one another for a few hours. I want to sit there and throw back drinks all night, feel the weight of Patrick's arm around me and the softness of the girls' heads in my lap when they start to get tired. I want familiar things. I want to tell funny stories about Conor. I want Oli to tell joke after joke, most of which are rubbish, not really caring if anyone laughs.

There's some guilt as well, sitting beneath the surface and putting me on edge. Some things I can't shake. The horror in Patrick's voice the night he found him, the mantra that he wouldn't leave alone no matter how much I tried to calm him... *I should have known... why didn't I know... I should have known he was in trouble.* And the thing is, I feel like I did know. In a way. I knew Sophie was gone for good, but I'd nodded along when Patrick said it was probably too early to tell and that it might get better. And I knew Conor was underwater on the finances for the site, and that he had gone to visit Sophie and seemed frantic and erratic. Sophie would text me updates, filled with bile and fury.

I said all this to Patrick that night, my own confession creeping into the space between his animal howls, his body seeming to contort with pain and shock. And he did what he does. He told me not to worry, that I was being stupid, that Sophie had probably said something awful to him, that I should probably message her and tell her what had happened, that she wasn't picking up anyone else's calls. I loved him for that, but there have still been moments where I wonder if I should have spoken up earlier, if maybe that might have set a different chain of events in motion. But how fine grained can you get with suffering? We are all just trying to muddle through, just about managing to stay balanced. So it didn't surprise me that one of us fell off the high wire, not really, not deep down.

I messaged Sophie that night . . . *thanks for letting me know.* And then nothing. After the fourth unanswered message, I'd gone to see her. Dragged the girls on three buses to get to the new-build cul-de-sac where she was living with her parents. But something in her had frozen over, repeating . . . *I know this already . . . why have you come all this way to tell me things that I already know* . . . Clutching at Sean relentlessly, pulling him close, unable to tear her eyes away from him for long enough to look at me properly. A holy child to her, wreathed in icon gold. A whole world. I told her over and over to come and stay with us for a few days while things got sorted out, but I knew she wouldn't. It was too late; in her head she was an ocean away. She wanted to breathe new air. Or maybe just breathe. And deep down, I got it. If you feel like your life is on fire, what else is there to do but warm your hands with the heat and then walk away?

I think I'd known that Conor had been physical with her, but had wanted to imagine it as something small and containable, an argument that got out of hand, pushing her away and not knowing his own strength, that type of thing, something with plausible deniability. But standing in front of her that night, I'd felt all of a sudden that it was much worse, that he had shown her something she couldn't unsee. If I'm honest, there had been a part of me that hadn't wanted to know the full extent, or to have it confirmed. But when it finally came out I could see that it mattered to Sophie that I heard it, that I witnessed it being made into words. And it mattered to me too. It mattered . . . *what the fuck do you think, Shiv? . . . don't pretend you didn't know how he could be . . . he lost it completely . . . there was nothing behind his eyes . . . I didn't think he would ever stop.* So when everyone was speculating about whether she'd turn up today, I knew she wouldn't. Uncrossable water.

Towards the end of the night, people keep coming up to Patrick and thanking him for the reading. Nodding at Rian while they're at it . . . *thanks for today . . . no worries.* Before the music properly starts, there are occasional songs. A cluster of the oldest lads are already half cut and keep breaking into some of the old, sad ballads about valleys and heather and rovers. And then Bread and Roses, which happens every time you put these lads in the pub together for long enough . . . *our lives shall not be sweated, from birth until life closes . . . hearts starve as well as bodies . . . give us bread but give us roses . . .* I see Patrick silently mouthing the words, then scrunching his eyes shut. And then leaving the room before the song takes over him.

Later, there is dancing. The free bar is keeping the younger crowd here for longer than they planned. Taxis on to clubs getting rearranged and pushed back another hour. Good for them. It's nice to watch them move. It's a good thing to have a body and be able to live in it, even if it's only for a time.

Oli

In the days after Conor died, I stopped having dreams again. As I'd got clean they'd returned after years of being completely absent. They'd come back vivid and angry with colour, and then all of a sudden, a return to nothing. It sounds strange, but I think I actually saw them disappear. I watched the end of my dreaming happen. The final dream. A dream full of dry leaves, me above them, following them as they moved about the town on the wind. Watching them blow up against the brick and the steel of the site, their brittle greens and browns pressing up against the clay and the silver with a dry crunch. And then the fade. Slow at first and then to greyscale and then to a distant blur and then finally to nothing. Since then, dreamless night after dreamless night. And now today we lower his body into the ground. I wonder what they are sealing in there with him; it can't just be air, ready to grow fetid over the years, something else must get trapped when they close the lid. The unvarnished, plain wood lid. I told Rian that over and over again . . . *I know the varnished one is nicer . . . but Conor had a real thing about shiny wood.*

It's hard to know what to do with yourself at these things. I mean, fuck, it's hard to know what to do with yourself full stop. But funerals are especially bad for it. I keep myself busy telling the girls jokes, gurning at them, pulling faces and finding an old pack of cards behind the bar to do some magic tricks with. I only know a couple of basic tricks I learned as a kid, probably only a few years older than the girls are now. But those things never get tired, not really. It's always exciting to feel like somebody is reading your mind, or that it's possible to make things appear and disappear whenever you want them to.

And being around the girls is useful in other ways, too. It gives us all a good excuse to lie about what happened to Conor, to pretend it is them we are sparing by calling it an accident. They stop us slipping and starting a conversation none of us are brave enough to finish. And they are a safeguard from anyone who might come over half pissed and start asking us about what it was like when we found him. Not that I know what it was like. It's not the type of thing you can really know. All I can remember is that his mouth was open so wide that I could see the metal fillings in his back teeth, like coins in the bottom of an old wallet. And I can remember that my tongue automatically lurched back in my mouth in response, running over years of holes and cracks and neglect.

And I can remember knowing, all at once, that heaven was definitely made of water. That it wasn't somewhere you go. That it was something formless that fills you up. Something that takes the shape of whatever it fills.

Throughout the day, a few of the lads start asking about the site. Asking if I know what will happen to it, whether I have spoken to Rian. They think I have some sort of inside line, or some sort of authority. And maybe I do, which is a really weird thought. I keep wanting to ask Rian, but I can't decide if today is totally the wrong time to do it, or whether in some perverse way it is exactly the right moment, when the implications of it are staring us all so squarely in the face. I'd totally get it if he wanted to just tear the whole thing down, I really would. I'd pick up a sledgehammer and join in myself, if that's what he really wanted. But there's no denying that the lads need it, they need the work. And so do I. I need the work as well. I've been measuring my life out at that place, its pull keeping me steady. And it's done something to me, watching the thing come to life so slowly, each choice, each brick and rivet only making sense weeks or months down the line. I think I'm getting sick of things happening fast. Everything has felt too quick for too long. I like that the site seemed to take forever to grow.

I've been back there once since Conor died. The place felt strange, empty. Empty in that way that only happens when you aren't sure if something is ever coming back. It had only been a week or so, but it had already started to take on the air of something abandoned. Someone had graffitied one of the cabins, and I knew if it didn't get cleaned that more and more would come. I walked the perimeter, the way Conor had started doing in the weeks before all this happened, taking things in as best I could, trying to see what he saw. I walked into the middle of the site, grabbed at the pulleys and let the blue rope slide through my hands over and over again. And then I climbed the scaffold, wanting to remember what it felt like to be up there, as high as a house, where there was always more cold and always more wind.

At some point Rian tells me that we used to have school discos here, in this same hall. That doesn't feel right to me, I think this is a different hall entirely. The one we had our school discos in had that really rough, itchy carpet with bevelled lines down the middle. I remember it really vividly, because I once spent weeks learning how to do a basic break-dance spin to impress the girls in our year. But then when the disco happened I realised it wouldn't work on the fucking carpet. When I tell Rian this he laughs. Puts his arm over my shoulder. Tells me that was twenty years ago, that they've probably changed the carpet a few times since then. But I'm not sure. That doesn't feel true to me. I feel like sometimes you are in a building and you can just tell that it has always been that way, that the floor has always been solid, that it has never suffered the indignity of an ugly carpet.

Later, there are songs. Old workers' songs and fighting

songs and songs about home that confuse those who are too young to know which home the songs are talking about. It's been a long day and people are already getting a bit edgy on the drink. Some want to let loose, to celebrate Conor, to celebrate not being dead themselves. Others seem offended by that, not liking the way the ritual is falling to pieces in front of their eyes. Rian brings over a tray of shorts, at least two for each of us. I down mine one after another, letting them burn my throat. The girls are asleep on Shiv's lap. I want to leave. I badly want to leave. Tonight feels like the end of a party that has gone on for way too long.

Five

Patrick

It's been a year. What happens to a body that has been underground for a year? What eats and erodes it, which parts of it start to disappear first?

Grim thoughts like that all day, fixated on flesh and bone, but trying to shake them as I push open the door to the pub. An anniversary drink, a chance to raise a glass to Conor. Rian suggested it and it seemed impossible to say no. I didn't ask any of the questions I wanted to ask . . . *are we intending to do this every year until one year nobody can make it and we all feel a bit embarrassed? . . . what happens when someone else dies? . . . do we do the same for them, or do we just do it for the first one of us who falls?* I tried to get Shiv to come tonight; I was more than happy to stay in with the girls. I even suggested that if she didn't want to go on her own we could get a babysitter, or ask her mom to come around. She insisted we couldn't afford that, and that her mom wasn't up to it any more, both of which were true enough, but I also know she was glad to have an excuse to stay at home.

A year since Conor died. A year since Conor was alive. A year since Conor killed himself. A year since the funeral. In the first few minutes nobody can decide which of those are the right words, each person seemingly having settled on their own preference in private. People who have known each other for years, feeling each other out all over again. Round after round of treading on eggshells until someone finds exactly the right tone and the stories and the laughs start to flow. Oli hasn't turned up, or not yet at least. I don't blame him; he's been a bit withdrawn these past few months, flinching away every time someone mentions Conor.

Round after round of pints, lads who worked with Conor raising sombre toasts and some of the older lads figuring out why we are all here and coming over to nod and pass on their sympathy . . . *seemed a good sort . . . you all have a good night eh* . . . It's been ages since I've been out like this, but I'm starting to get the hang of it again, some familiar light switching on inside me. If we're going to do it, let's do it properly. I don't want pints, I want shorts and shots and powder and pills, fuck it, pretend we are other people, somewhere else, some other time.

The night of the funeral, right before we were getting ready to leave, Oli told me he had stopped dreaming. He seemed a bit embarrassed to tell me, going on about watching all the colour leak away. At the time I didn't get why he was so bothered about it; I told him I go weeks without dreaming, or without remembering them at least. But in the months afterwards his words kept coming back to me. It was as if he'd put a curse on the place or something; whatever had drained the colour from his dreams had slipped out of his head and started sucking it out of the real world as well, draining the grass and the sky and the buildings, the whole estate fixed in alabaster like a death mask. I kept telling myself that it was only in my head, that one day I'd snap out of it and everything would leap back into colour like flowers after the spring has spat out the first shock of rain. But it didn't quite happen like that. It came back slowly. Falling asleep and remembering that I had seen something red that day. And the next day a dull blue, washed out to almost grey. And then finally, yellow, the last to come back before things felt normal again. I wasn't entirely sure if things had come back properly, though. Or if the colours had returned almost imperceptibly less bright. I wondered if this was the first time it had happened to me, or whether the world was actually much brighter once, but had got ever so slightly dimmer each time someone I loved died and I just hadn't been paying enough attention to notice.

So that's how it is now. The same life. Except Conor is not in it. And something weird may or may not have happened to the colours. Oh, and my job is harder. Because I'm a year older and because I can't ride any routes that take me past the park. The first few times I had to do it I was O.K., but then I started to get these fucking awful flashbacks. Not every time, but often enough that even the thought of it happening shook me up. I'd see the light of the ambulance cutting across the grass and lighting up his face, the water already bulging underneath his skin, as if it needed to escape. As if it had somewhere else it needed to be.

Tonight, thankfully, Rian seems to have the same idea as me. He looked halfway fucked when he turned up, and I am grateful when he reaches under the table and pushes a plastic packet and a rolled-up note into my hand. Later, he corners me. Far gone enough to want to talk. It's happened a few times over the last year or so and I usually manage to shut it down before he makes me angry. We can't talk our distance away, I keep telling him. Just leave it be. I don't want to hear any more of him saying he didn't mean it and how fucked up he was and how he wished he'd never said anything. I don't want to hear it because it makes me want to scream at him. It makes me want to say . . . *yes, but that's the whole fucking point isn't it, you prick . . . and you can't see that . . . even if you didn't mean it, you were still willing to throw a fucking bomb into my life . . . our life . . . just to make you feel better . . . Shiv and the girls are the only good thing I have and you fucking risked it for your greed . . . you careless fuck . . . you careless greedy fuck . . . sad because your money wasn't enough . . . because your massive weird empty flat wasn't enough . . . because sad little Rian got bored of looking at the river and bored of ripping people off . . . fuck you . . .*

I say none of this. I ask for another line.

Rian

From this distance, it almost feels like everything happened on the same day. In my head I ran away, moved back here, fucked up my friendship with Patrick, and then Conor died. All at once. The days in between have collapsed. And every moment since has been soaked with the sadness of it, with a type of panic that you have to work hard to stop from overtaking you.

In the weeks after the funeral, I could feel all the old language leaking in. Talking like my nan. Curses and marks and omens and auguries. Maybe I dragged something evil back here with me, fished something wretched out of the river and carried it home along the motorway in my ridiculous car.

Too much time alone, trying to build something that looked like a passable life. Building it the way everyone else builds theirs: by repeating a set of actions and concerns so often that you eventually forget that doing them is a choice. I started by going to sleep at about the same time every night, making coffee at about the same intervals throughout the day, checking the same few websites and reading the same few newspapers. It wasn't much, but it was enough to build on. Once those things stopped feeling like choices, I started adding other things to the pattern. A rich life by tiny increments. I started walking to the centre of the estate every lunchtime, haunting the place like a punctual ghost. And buying things to fill my house, taking an interest in which objects were the right objects. Not minding if the objects matched, just whether each individual object felt right in and of itself. It turned out the choosing actually did matter. And then finally, music. Racks and racks of records and discs. After years of not caring, hungry for all of the sound. All at once.

I don't know what the idea behind the choosing is. I think I have the vague sense that if I choose the right things, the right cups and vases and seats and pictures, then at some point I will have reached the end of the game and managed to make a home. And that once you have done that, once you have made a home, then you can open the door and the whole world will rush in. Recently, I keep thinking about my old man, and wondering if he did something like this. Did he run his hands over sets of knives and forks, weigh them in his fist and then put them down again because they weren't quite right? We had cutlery growing up, so it must have come from somewhere, but maybe someone just gave them to us, or maybe he just got the cheapest set that still looked like they might be able to cut up some meat a couple of times a week? What I'm saying is, I've started to ache for not knowing him properly, for not paying attention. For not asking him how you make a life.

The site is staying open. After Conor died I couldn't stand to look at the place, wanted to pull it down or maybe just leave it hanging there, unfinished, a monument to bad decisions and waste. But when I spoke to Oli he told me it would be brutal to do that after so many of them had put so much into it, day after day. He also said that going there regularly had helped him and that it would be good to finish what we started. That was good enough for me, so the thing is getting finished. I've got someone new in to oversee it and have told him to take as long as it takes. I don't need to make money on the thing; I never really expected to anyway. He just has to make sure that they are built properly. If we are going to clutter up the sky and annoy all the old lads in the Trident, the least we can do is build something that might last a lifetime or two. Patrick is pushing me to go further with it. When I asked him if he had ideas, he was a hundred miles an hour about co-ops and residents' associations, community rates not market rates, and all the rest of it. It's not really my thing, but he probably does have a point, there are plenty of people around here living in absolute shitholes and being ripped off for the privilege. It was probably the closest thing to a real conversation we've had since I came back.

Tonight we are drinking to remember Conor. Not that he has been forgotten yet, but we all know it can happen, and that it usually does if you give it enough time. Vivid people become vivid memories and then eventually even the memories start to lose their form. Sadnesses get buried by other sadnesses until it gets hard to see through all of the sediment. Think of all the people we knew as kids. How many loomed large for us every day and now we can't picture their face or we end up bickering in the pub about what their surname was. Me, Oli, Patrick, Conor, Shiv, we thought we were different from our parents, more alive somehow, braver maybe. But we were wrong about that. We are making all the same mistakes, letting go of all the same things, one by one. But that doesn't mean we can't toast our myth, tell some stories about all the ways we were going to be. Something doesn't have to have been real for it to be worth keeping alive. So we are getting fucked up for Conor tonight. And for the memory of a time when it was hard to imagine we wouldn't all live for ever. Forget that the party is basically over; if we can't have it as a life, we will have it as a ceremony instead.

The night goes. I can feel myself being needy with Patrick, forcing things. I'm too fucked to stop my mouth. It feels like the blow is making my actual spine sweat. Not sweat running down my spine, sweat coming out of my spine. Can that be right? . . . *you don't get it mate . . . I'd do anything . . . I want you to hit me . . . mark my face . . . break my ribs if you like . . . beat my body ink blue . . . I don't give a fuck . . . get it out of your system . . .* I don't tell him about the morning a few months ago when I took my shoes and socks off and stepped into the lake for a second so I could feel how the water would have felt for Conor. But how instead it made me remember that time he fell in and we all laughed. Why didn't it occur to me that he would have been scared?

Patrick isn't having any of it. I can feel I am making things worse. He is reacting the way a dog does when it can tell you are desperate for its affection. Last orders. I try a new approach... *let's go on somewhere else... and let's go and get Oli while we are at it... if we're going to drink instead of talking about our feelings we should at least do it with him...* Patrick has taken enough of the drugs I brought to not argue with this plan. He nods, asks for another line, and then we leave.

Oli

Three heavy knocks, the long shrill of the doorbell and then the sound of two laughing bodies slumped against the door. I'm not asleep, but I am in bed, and have been for hours. It's something I have learned over the past year: the earlier you get into bed, the sooner you are likely to go to sleep. And the sooner you go to sleep, the more sleep you get before you have to wake up. This is especially true if you try to read, or listen to one of those radio programmes where old men with incredibly deep voices talk about rivers or bridges or trade routes. If I do that, then usually sleep will take me within the hour. I wish I had figured this out twenty years ago. For some reason I had been labouring under the illusion that sleep came whenever it was ready and there was nothing you could do to hurry it along. But I messed up the system tonight, lying awake and wondering if I should have gone to Conor's anniversary drinks, whether it was an awful thing to do to spend the night alone instead. I messed up the system and now it's too late. These two idiots banging on my door and me with no excuse not to answer.

It's not just the sleeping thing that I wish I had known twenty years ago. There's a whole fucking list of things. Basic things that have only recently begun to come into focus. Such as the fact that your head tends to hurt less if you drink water. And the fact that fruit is actually really delicious if you get a piece that has been in the sun for just the right amount of time. And also that there are other ways of living. That war or oblivion aren't the only options, and that there are moods available to me other than blank and euphoric. I mean, on some level, I've obviously always known these things. They feel incredibly familiar to me. But they had been hovering out of view for so long that there is something startling about encountering them all over again.

And I'm better for knowing them. Everything is better these days. Easier, slower, less jagged and frayed. And the breathing. As if my lungs were double the size they were when I was using all the time. What do people do with all of that air? I've only slipped back twice in the last year, both times just after Conor died. But other than that, I think I'm done. I can't know for sure, obviously, but after all these years, something feels like it has dislodged. I'm full up. Not hungry for it. And the ending feels so different from the beginning. At the beginning I could feel my life changing, second by second, as the needle pushed through my skin. The feeling of it just hung there like thunder about to break, or like a heavy flag about to drop and signal the start of a race. But the ending feels different. Less solid. You can sense that the race is over. But there is no flag and no thunder. Or not that I can see from here.

A memory. Wandering back from a house I had been in for days, splayed out and drifting in between fixes. The time of year when it can be almost sunrise but still nowhere near morning. A part of the city I knew well enough, but in the state I was in it looked like a familiar TV programme on a detuned television. And a dog. The least surprising looking dog, brown and small and simpering. The least surprising but still surprising. There in the world. On its own, dragging a thin red lead along in its wake. And I was high enough that I took it. I just picked up the dog and took him home. Carried him through the streets all ratty and bug eyed and put him next to me on my sofa while I blacked out for god knows how long. That same stolen dog is sitting at the end of my bed right now, grunting occasionally in his sleep. I never felt guilty for taking that dog, not once. So there's a silver lining. If I hadn't wasted all those years of my life as an addict then I wouldn't have stolen a dog that it later turned out I really loved.

And these days there is the site. The slow rhythm of it and the knowing it will be there day after day. The lines and the shapes and the heft of it. It's the type of work that tells you straight away if you are doing something wrong. If the brick isn't lying flush, you can see it and so you do it again, and you keep doing it until it is right. Just this constant physical feedback telling you how you are messing up and how to fix it. Something incredibly reassuring about that. About not having to wait months or years to know if you've made the right choice about something. Also, I think Patrick will end up doing something good with the houses. He's got ideas for them and I know Rian will listen when it comes down to it.

Doorbell again and more laughter . . . *get out of bed you prick . . . we know you're there . . . we're going out.* And the two of them, standing there. The semi-delirious smiles you only get when you are seriously high. I wanted to avoid tonight, avoid the stories and fumbling. But there's no avoiding this . . . *let's go . . . let's go . . . socks and shoes on . . .* There is something in it. Some joy in it. The stupidity of them both, collapsing into the back of the taxi, still not really talking but holding on to one another's shoulders and elbows for balance. And it is good to be out at night, moving along the black roads and chasing somewhere that might still have a light on for us. Good to be here, next to these bodies, and good to dance. Always good to dance. Before things went bad, before the flag came down and started the race, I was O.K. at it as well. If it hadn't been for that weird carpet, I would have even pulled off that spin at the school disco all those years ago. Maybe everything would have unfolded differently if I had. I imagine things would have looked strange from down there, watching the ceiling turn above me.

Rian

There is something about being crushed into the back of a taxi with people you love. It has never stopped feeling like an adventure. Even if you've done it a thousand times, even if you know that the sensible thing to do would be to tell the driver to turn around and take you home, to quit while you are ahead. The unnatural ways your bodies collide and slide over one another every time the car takes a tight corner, the tangle of legs, the unfamiliar songs, hearing adverts on the radio that seem to beam in from decades ago, an age when people decided to buy kitchens or patios or double glazing because some local maniac screamed about crazy deals and one-time offers. It's the point of the night with the most possibility, before the jigsaw pieces get fixed and you start to see the final picture.

The club doesn't want to let us in. Only an hour and a half until it closes, last entry already long gone and enough experience on the door to realise that we must be fairly wrecked to try to get in at this time of night. It takes fifty quid to the bouncer and a bunch of undignified promises about being on our best behaviour to win them round. Down the stairs, one room to the left and another to the right, the one place in the whole building where the sounds from each are bleeding into each other. Something thicker, bassier, more obliterating to the left. And to the right, something more familiar, lighter, vocals and hi hats and hand claps. Patrick immediately palms the drugs from me and heads to the toilet. Oli makes the decision and leads the way to the room on the right . . . *actual songs mate . . . you're not dragging me out to sit in a fucking cave with a bunch of dribbling pill heads . . .*

Three pints to the corner booth, where I can watch Oli dance and wait for Patrick to come back from the toilet. Oli is straight into the middle of things, barely moving his legs and feet but his arms and shoulders rocking in time with the music. At first he is hitting every beat and then after a couple of minutes I notice that he has started finding the time in between the beats, punctuating the rhythm with his hands and his elbows. He's a fucking bundle of energy. When Patrick sits down, I slide his pint over and nod towards Oli. Patrick is watching him too now. Smiling. Impossible not to. There are moments when the light catches him and it is twenty years ago and the boy is still the most beautiful thing you have ever seen. I wonder if Patrick thinks the same. The white pulse hits his face and scatters into fragments. New light on new glass.

And then I see her. Or think I see her. Over Oli's shoulder, head tipped back, mouth open in silent laughter. It looks as though she is roaring at the sky, trying to get its attention. Trying to make the universe be less incurious. How fucked am I? . . . *Patrick, mate, am I seeing things or is that Sophie over there, behind Oli . . . no, to the left a bit, by the pillar . . . it can't be, right? . . . she wouldn't be here tonight . . . of all the fucking nights?* But Patrick is sure it isn't her, adamant she would never go out around here, and when she finally turns and faces us front on, I can see that he is right. It isn't her. Seeing things. Seeing ghosts. Is that what it will be now, memories of Conor everywhere, leaking out of the walls, shadows catching you out when you aren't paying attention? Everything an echo of an older life until the echoes are the only sound you hear. She walks right past our booth. Up close she can't be any older than about nineteen. Really fucked. That's how fucked I am. Really fucked.

I can't hear Patrick from across the table, so I move around and sit next to him. An hour in and we are shouting in one another's ears, sentences half finished and half heard . . . *I keep thinking I should buy the Trident and turn it into a karaoke bar . . . they already hate me in there so I might as well go the whole way . . . or maybe they'd love it . . . few power ballads can really liven up a game of dominoes . . .*

And I don't want the talking to end, so I don't say any of the things I want to say. Even though they are always there, trying to edge their way between us.

I don't say that I lied, and that I did love her. Even though it was only for a bit. Or that maybe I still love her. Or that I still think about it all the time. Not about her exactly, but about the feeling of it, and how that feeling seemed to be something that actually mattered. Even though it was only for a bit. Or that even though I keep telling him that it was nothing, it wasn't nothing. It was something. And for a moment at least, it was maybe everything. And that matters. Even though it was only for a bit. That matters.

I don't say that I can still remember the shadow between her hair and her cheek.

Or the home of her neck.

And I don't say that I need him to forgive me.

Or that I know now that you can't always have the things you want.

And that there are some things you don't do.

And I don't keep saying . . . *surely you get that? surely you get that?*

So I say other things instead.

. . . might as well finish the job . . . karaoke at the Trident it is . . . and drum and bass every Sunday.

Patrick

When it comes to drinking, most people are like a dimmer switch, getting gradually darker or lighter by increments. But these days, I'm in the other category. Binary. The switch is either on or off. And when the switch is pressed, that's it, game over. I'll start chasing the night until I catch up with it and make it do what I need it to do. It doesn't happen often, but when it does, that's always how it goes. It goes the way it has to go. Suddenly ravenous for being alive.

Tonight is like that. I felt the switch get pressed back in the pub, and now I am throwing things on the fire, trying to make sure it doesn't go out before the morning arrives. My old man used to talk about early houses, pubs that would open at dawn to serve dock workers, milkmen and people finishing a nightshift. But I imagine there would have been other people there too. A handful in the corner who had stayed out late and now couldn't quite bear to go home, who at some point in the night had realised that they needed to see the sunrise. It's nice to think of those places, but I also know that it is probably for the best that we don't have them around here any more.

It's my greed that carries us out of the pub and has us knocking on Oli's front door, and it's my greed that means we end up in this shit club. I've always felt out of place in clubs, and that feeling doesn't get any less pronounced when you are the oldest person in there by at least a decade. But it's not all bad. We are still out; that's all that matters. The night is still happening. And it is good to hear music this loud, realising that songs I thought

I didn't like actually make much more sense at this volume. So I ease into it, into the beers and the lines and Rian talking in my ear at a hundred miles an hour. Let it all slide over me. And Oli, dancing and moving and rolling his head, making me think about words like fibreoptic and livewire. I swear to god, the fucker will probably outlive all of us, dance at all of our funerals. Let it slide all over me, wait for the oblivion of things.

And then the bell. The last orders. And then the lights... *you know what, Rian? ... bells and lights are heavy things ... symbols ... marking the passing ... something ending ... calling us up from the underworld and into the air.* So that's what we do. Fucked up and into the air. There will be no work tomorrow, or no work today, depending on how you draw your lines. Outside the club, Oli has his hands on someone's waist, his wrists still rake thin even though the rest of him has filled out recently. He leads her over to where Rian and I are standing ... *we're going to head off lads ... thanks for getting me out of bed.* He looks happy and alive. And we are fifteen again, watching him leave with the girl at the end of every party.

And then the bright, painful white of the newsagent strip light. And the hundreds of products, reds and blues and golds, shipped from every corner of the earth and then clustered here in this tiny space so there is always just the thing you want at just the time you want it. If I think about that for too long, about the flux and the flow and the hands and the bodies and the ships and the trucks, then I start to feel dizzy and disconnected. Just pay for the cans and then leave. Something to keep us going until the sun comes up, something cold to grip in our fists.

Rian and I walk up through the centre of the city, towards the cathedral. Straight past the taxi rank, cars lined up and fighting for the last few customers of the night. When we first started going out, it used to be the other way around, queues of people fighting to get a taxi to take them home. They'd never want to take us to where we were going. Mostly lads, to a place with a bad reputation. So we'd use Shiv as a decoy. She'd pretend she was going home alone and then the moment they'd agreed to take her, we'd all bundle in alongside her and split the fare between us. But even for kids from the estate, I doubt there is a need to fight for a taxi any more. A hundred cars in your phone and a line of them snaking around the corner, all happy for the fare. Rian is a few metres ahead of me, slaloming through the line of parked cars. He's a different shape these days, broader, rounder, prouder somehow. But he moves the same, eighteen and ready to jump in the first car that fell for our scam. The way watching somebody from a distance can collapse things, just for a second. A concertina, you at ten, you at twenty, you when you are long gone. And a hole where the present is supposed to be.

Something must have gone wrong with the cathedral. It's been years now, and it is still covered in scaffolding. Maybe there has been a public announcement and I just didn't notice. Maybe it was announced that we have all officially given up on finishing things, that we have entered the era of the perpetual repair, the skies always full of cranes and the buildings always jutting with metal supports in case they fall down and cause a lawsuit. The cathedral gives me the same feeling that the newsagent gave me. Dizzy to think of the hundreds of people who must have spent their entire life building it, shaving the stone and painting the glass. Who must have thought it was worth it, that it was a reasonable way to spend a life, making somewhere for people to sing and sit, somewhere for people to think about what they want and what they have lost. And a statue too, in the courtyard, watching over the whole thing. A statue that looks tired tonight. Tired of looking at scaffolding. Like it might be ready to give up the ghost and just start breathing, stretch out its stone arms. Too much effort to stay still for another two hundred years.

The last few drops from the can as the sky turns. Purple first and then finally orange. Rian is right, we should make a move, share a cab. And then I find myself saying it . . . *come back to ours if you like . . . get some breakfast before you crash . . . Molly and Freya will probably be up by then anyway and they'd be glad to see you . . . so will Shiv . . . just don't ask me if I'm fucking sure about it, because I'm obviously not sure . . . so don't ask.*

Rian has his eyes closed, lolled back against the headrest . . . *yeah, that would be really nice mate . . . let's do that.*

So we arc home, still too early for there to be many cars on the road. Empty enough that the buildings look unfamiliar as we speed past them, my own eyes closing now. And the final thoughts before the inside of my eyelids drench the world in red . . . there must be a better way than this . . . better ways to be together, better ways to spend our time. Better ways to spend the actual time of our actual life.

When we pull up to the flat, the driver knocks the glass to wake us.

SHIV

Patrick is out tonight. Anniversary drinks, a year since Conor's death. I couldn't go, or to be more precise, I didn't want to go. I didn't want to watch them fumble around, trying different words and different stories until they all found a rhythm and a tone they could agree on for the night. It's been painful to watch, these last few months, people who have known each other their whole lives trying to find a new way to exist now that something has finally ended. Now one of them has gone. All cradling their version of him, various degrees of sanitised and safe. They are learning what to leave behind and what to try to carry forward and save. The thing is, sometimes the answer is nothing. Sometimes it's less painful just to burn the boats.

Patrick hasn't figured that out yet; deep down he's the sort of person who thinks everything can be fixed, always has been.

But I've known that feeling over and over again, the sense of something shifting under me, inside me. The realisation that I need to leave parts of myself behind, in someone's bed, on a bus I never wanted to be on, at a hospital while some new life tore through me and everything changed for ever.

But I get that it's painful. I get why he doesn't want to do it. There are still days I wish I could go back in time and speak to every version of me that I didn't manage to save, every part of me that I had to leave behind. I'd tell every one of them the same thing. Sentimental maybe, but exactly what I needed to hear at the time . . . *I know you think you are fucking up . . . but you are way stronger than you think . . . don't worry, believe it or not, you make it through this . . . and you make it through the next thing too . . . and the thing after that . . . and guess what? you don't die . . . you just live . . . and then you live a bit more . . . and everything ends up more or less O.K.*

And there is another reason I didn't want to go tonight. Patrick doesn't know this yet, but I think there might be another baby. I haven't done a test, but I am pretty sure I'm right. I've started to get that same ache I had in my hips when I was pregnant with each of the girls, and the same type of dreams too. Dreams full of tiny mouths, stretched open and showing the blackness of their throats, trying to eat all of the sunlight, trying to struggle into life.

And I can feel myself wanting to pray again, my hands coming together at night. Me asking under my breath. Asking for the same thing I've been asking for since I was a teenager . . .

Dear god, please shelter me for long enough that this life can grow.

I know what will happen. I will tell Patrick there is another baby and we will talk for weeks about how there isn't enough money in the bank, or how there isn't enough space in the flat, or how there aren't enough hours in the day, or enough days in a life. And then soon enough, my stomach will start to arch and dome and stretch and that will be that. Everything will have changed all over again.

No sign of Patrick before I go to sleep, and no sign of him when I wake up either. Must have been a good night. Or a really bad one. Those are the only two types that go on until morning. Snooze the alarm twice and sprawl my legs over to Patrick's side of the bed, small stolen luxuries. And then coffee, taking out two mugs by force of habit but remembering just in time before I spoon in the dry granules.

I stand at the window with my coffee, the girls' muffled voices in the next room, and let the steam from the cup rise and hit my nose and cheeks. Same view every morning. Same place I've always known, all of the same shapes and silhouettes, stretched out over the horizon and up towards the park and the lake. The park and the lake that used to be the most beautiful part of the estate but that now we all avoid.

And the new flats in the distance. The only thing that has really changed. Jagged and angular and seeming to get bigger by the week. The old lads are sort of right about them, they do change the sky. As I watch them, they seem to be sucking in all of the oranges and the reds, breathing in the morning like a pair of heavy cement lungs. Keeping themselves alive. Knowing that there is always one more brick.

I see the taxi pull in. A delay while somebody pays the fare. And then two bodies. Two sets of eyes squinting up and seeing me at the window.

And white sun. On skin. On metal. On water.

Acknowledgements

All books are collective efforts, and this one is no different. It wouldn't exist without the patience, talent, kindness and belief of so many people. I'm lucky and blessed.

Special thanks go to my agent, Clare Conville and the wider C&W team for their consistent belief in the book, and in me. And also to Anna Kelly and all at Abacus and Little, Brown. Without Anna's vision for this book, it would have been something entirely different, and something considerably worse—thank you for seeing so clearly and so often what I was unable to.

Thank you to the Society of Authors for providing a work-in-progress grant in support of this novel.

Thank you to all of my friends (Delinquents and Former Delinquents in particular) for their unending supply of entertainment and love.

Thank you to my family, especially Olivia and Patrick, I know I am not always an easy person to love, so the fact that you do is a genuine gift.

And lastly, thank you to the people, places and policies that sustained me as a kid; to Birmingham, to Shard End, to the schools and the teachers and the libraries, to the mates and the corner shops and the youth clubs, the Sunday league teams, community centres, EMA grants and free lunches, the union settlements, the marches, the scholarships and the social security payments . . . to public luxury . . . which is the only luxury that matters.